IT WAS AS IF SHE'D NEVER BEEN KISSED BEFORE.

She felt Cal's hard body pressing against her, and it was useless to pretend that she didn't want to press back against him . . . in fact, it proved impossible to pretend anything. She simply reacted, opening her mouth to receive his kisses, moaning his name, catching her breath when his hands moved over her, stirring her responses to wildfire.

Never had she lost her head with a man—but now she couldn't help herself. She heard her own voice pleading with him as if in a dream.

"Cal . . . please, please . . . I want you so."

CANDLELIGHT ECSTASY ROMANCES™

WINTER WINDS

Jackie Black

A CANDLELIGHT ECSTASY ROMANCE™

Published by
Dell Publishing Co., Inc.
1 Dag Hammarskjold Plaza
New York, New York 10017

ISBN: 0–440–19528–4

Printed in the United States of America
First printing—February 1982

Dear Reader:

In response to your enthusiasm for Candlelight Ecstasy Romances™, we are now increasing the number of titles per month from three to four.

We are pleased to offer you sensuous novels set in America, depicting modern American women and men as they confront the provocative problems of a modern relationship.

Throughout the history of the Candlelight line, Dell has tried to maintain a high standard of excellence, to give you the finest in reading pleasure. It is now and will remain our most ardent ambition.

Editor
Candlelight Romances

CHAPTER ONE

The car died so suddenly, Janna barely had time to pull over to the shoulder of the highway. Once stopped, she stared in annoyed perplexity at the darkened dashboard. For the last half hour or so, she'd noticed that the head-lights were gradually dimming, and she'd planned to stop at the nearest service station to find out why. But service stations were few and far between on this lonely stretch of road, and now it was too late!

Damn! Janna slapped the steering wheel impotently. She didn't know enough about the inner workings of an automobile to even guess at what the problem might be, and after several futile attempts to restart the motor, she realized she was well and truly stuck. Glancing at the glowing dial of her watch, she saw it was eleven o'clock, and she cursed her own stupidity. Why hadn't she stopped at a motel in that last little town instead of barreling on down the road into the emptiness of a frigid Wyoming night! It wasn't as though she didn't have plenty of time. She wasn't due to report in at her new job for two days. But there was no use crying about it now. She hadn't been tired, so she hadn't stopped—and now she was paying for it.

She peered out the car window at the black night, quelling a shiver of anxiety. It was beginning to snow—she could just make out the wet flakes on the glass in front of her—and the wind was picking up enough to rock even the solid bulk of the car. Janna quickly abandoned the idea of trying to walk for help. It was miles to the next town and miles from the last one she'd passed through. Better to stay in the shelter of the car than to risk the freezing temperature outside. Even if there were a farmhouse nearby, she could easily miss it unless it were set close to the road and had lights to show the way.

Janna shivered again, as much from apprehension as from the cold that was already invading the interior of the car, and hoped desperately that someone would come by. But she hadn't seen another car for ages. It might be hours before another traveler spotted her, and even then they might not stop.

She caught herself up short and shook her head in impatience at her own morbid thoughts, chiding herself for giving in to panic so quickly. As another shiver racked her even through the protection of her car coat, she reached into the backseat for the blanket and pillow her brother had insisted she bring along. Normally, his cautious nature irritated her, but now she blessed him for his foresight. She would have liked some of the coffee she had brought along in a thermos, but caution dictated that she save it for later. The colder it got, the more she'd need any warmth she could find. So, instead, she wrapped herself in the blanket and rested her head against the pillow after propping it up against the window. She wanted to stay awake in case someone came by. She'd have to move fast if she saw headlights, or they might pass her up.

For a while, Janna contented herself with humming snatches of songs, making a game of trying to remember the words of ones she liked. The radio was dead, there was no light to read by, and she had to keep awake. Besides, it was better than letting her thoughts drift back over the painful circumstances that had brought her into this predicament. But it wasn't long before the thoughts she was trying to avoid took hold of her mind, blotting out the cold and everything else with ruthless persistence.

Oh, Frank, she thought with despair. Why did you do it? She didn't know why she kept asking the question over and over when the answer was obvious. He'd simply preferred Mellie when all was said and done. Mellie—Janna's oldest friend—and now Frank's wife. Janna only wished Frank had discovered his love for Mellie before asking Janna to marry him. Then maybe she wouldn't be sitting here in the wilds of Wyoming agonizing over a love that was lost to her forever.

Closing her eyes wearily, Janna willed herself to turn off this useless rehashing of a hopeless situation. She was doing all she could to forget. A new job, a new state—new faces and contacts. Now if she could only find a new outlook in her own mind.

An hour passed. Her thoughts of Frank were mercifully gone. She'd jerked awake several times, but eventually her eyes closed for good and she slept peacefully, uncaring that the snow was building up inexorably on the windshield of the car while the temperature dropped steadily. Outside the window the wind gained strength and howled around the car with increasing ferocity, and still Janna slept, wrapped in a cocoon of forgetfulness.

At first Janna thought the persistent tapping on the window was part of her dream. She stirred restlessly, clutching the blanket closer to her. It was so cold! But then

11

the tapping was accompanied by the sound of a muffled voice, and gradually the words penetrated her consciousness.

"Open up in there! Are you all right? Come on, open the door!"

Janna opened her eyes, and turning her head, she could make out a dark shape peering in at her. Still half asleep, she struggled to untangle herself from the folds of the blanket. "Just a minute," she called hoarsely, and then louder, "I'm trying to get up!"

Fumbling at the blanket with cold-stiffened fingers, she was finally able to free herself enough to reach back and unlock the car door. Immediately, it was pulled open from outside, and a gust of snow and wind blew in on her from around the tall figure who stood there.

"Are you all right?" She couldn't see the man's features, but his voice was reassuringly deep and strong, although it held a note of impatience.

"I'm fine, I think," she said groggily, her own voice mumbly with sleep.

"Are you the only one in there?" Now he sounded slightly incredulous.

"Yes, and I'm so glad you're here," and suddenly Janna was wide awake and showing her relief by grasping one of her rescuer's hands where it rested on the steering wheel as he leaned into the car to talk to her out of the wind. "Can you help me get my car started? It just died, and I don't . . ."

Janna got no further as the man withdrew his hand from her grip and grasped her elbow with his other hand, pulling her toward him. "Forget the car!" The impatience was stronger now. "Get out of there and into my Jeep!"

Janna resisted, a faint resentment stirring at his high-handedness. "But, I . . ."

"No buts!" He was emphatic. "Can't you see we're in the middle of a blizzard? I figure we've got about half an hour before this road is completely impassable. Now are you coming or do I leave you here to freeze?"

Janna hesitated. Was it wise to put herself completely into the hands of a stranger? But the next moment another blast of cold wind blew in through the open door, and for the first time, she noticed how badly the weather had deteriorated. That decided her.

"All right, all right," she said ungraciously as he pulled on her arm again. "Just let me get my handbag and a suitcase." He stood back as she gathered up her purse and gloves and then removed her keys from the ignition. She held out the keys to the stranger. "Can you get my bag out of the trunk for me?" She flinched at the audible curse that greeted her words. She hadn't wanted to ask him to do it, but she wasn't sure she could stand upright in that wind on her numbed legs long enough to do it herself. And they might be stranded for several days. She needed that bag!

He grabbed the keys out of her hand and left her, and Janna struggled to get out of the car. Once outside, she found she could stand, but her legs weren't reliable, so she clung to the side of the car to wait for help. The Jeep looked a formidable distance away in her condition, although it was only a few yards up the road.

The stranger was back so quickly, he took her by surprise. "Come on," he said roughly, beckoning with his head in the direction of the Jeep. His hands were full with her overnight bag and suitcase, and he started off without looking back to see if she was following him.

Janna took a step forward and knew she wasn't going

13

to be able to make it. The wind almost knocked her down, and her feet were all pins and needles. She clung helplessly to the car, buffeted by wind and snow and watched the man dump her bags in the back of his Jeep and turn to look for her. Then he retraced his steps, and as he came up to her, she shouted at him above the howling wind. "I'm sorry—my legs are numb!"

She thought she saw him shake his head, and thinking he hadn't heard her explanation, she was opening her mouth to try again when he reached to pick her up in his arms so swiftly, she was surprised into silence. As he carried her to his Jeep, she wondered resentfully why he couldn't have just offered her his arm. But he had her in the other vehicle so quickly, she realized his way made more sense. If he'd tried to help her stumble along, they'd still be out there in the cold, instead of which she was already feeling the faint waves of warmth from the heater in the Jeep.

Oh, that feels good, she thought shiveringly as the man beside her began to ease the Jeep out onto the road. He drove carefully and skillfully through the piles of snow drifting about on the highway, picking up speed gradually. Janna wondered how he could see to drive. The wipers on her side were proving less than adequate in keeping the snow pushed away, but somehow she felt an inexplicable faith in this stranger, despite his brusque manner.

Glancing at him obliquely, she saw that he was concentrating wholly on the task, and she kept quiet, not wanting to disturb that concentration. But she studied him all the same. He had on a large Western hat, and his coat collar was pulled up around his chin, so that she couldn't see much of his face except for a well-shaped nose. He was tall, and from the way he'd carried her with such ease, he must have the strength to match his height.

Suddenly, he turned and flashed her a brief glance. Janna caught her breath. The light of the dash was dim, but it was bright enough for her to see that this man was a person to be reckoned with. His expression was hard—almost ruthless—and he made no attempt to hide the fact that he held her in contempt. But apart from that brief glance, he didn't say anything to her, and indeed, he ignored her as he turned back to his driving.

Janna slowly let out her breath, grateful for the respite. She was in no state to spar with a total stranger, and somehow she knew that however brief their acquaintance turned out to be, she and this man were going to spar. But not now. Fortunately, he had his hands full for the present.

As the warmth relaxed her, Janna began to recover some of her natural spirit, and with the spirit came a certain amount of resentment. What right had this arrogant male to treat her so disparagingly? Did he resent the fact that he'd had to rescue her? Perhaps he thought she had no business traveling alone being a mere woman?

The man filling her thoughts slowed the Jeep and peered through the snow-coated windshield as if searching for something, then made a quick turn to the right off the highway, causing the wheels to slide sickeningly in a skid. He maneuvered the Jeep skillfully and righted the vehicle, then picked up speed onto the narrow lane ahead. Janna relaxed her grip on the door and let out the breath she'd been holding unconsciously, reflecting that her nerves really couldn't take much more.

"What the hell are you doing out here alone at this time of night?" The man spoke to her so abruptly that Janna jumped. "If you have to travel, haven't you got sense enough to stop when it gets dark?" He was flicking glances at her as he spoke but still reserved most of his attention for the road ahead.

Janna's temper rose at the criticism. Was he going to make no attempt to be politely civil? But just as quickly as it came, her anger died. After all, the man was helping her out of a tight spot. It was just possible she owed him her life. So she answered him reasonably, keeping her voice neutral.

"I wasn't tired when I came through the last town. And I didn't realize I was going to have car trouble . . . or that there was going to be a blizzard."

Janna waited for him to say something in reply, but he only shook his head impatiently and continued to drive. Piqued at his silence, she decided to try a little charm, although she knew she couldn't come up to her usual standard in these circumstances.

"I want to thank you," she started, and somehow it came out all wrong. Her voice was high pitched and strained. She thought disgustedly that she sounded almost hysterical.

He gave her a quick, concerned look. "You're not going to pieces on me, are you? We're almost there."

Janna shrugged resignedly. Now he would think she was an overly emotional as well as a stupid female. Clearing her throat, she answered him.

"No. It's just that if you hadn't come along . . ." She left the rest unsaid. He knew what might have happened better than she did. He lived here.

"Forget it," he said shortly. "Anyone out here would have done the same."

Janna gave up trying to talk to him. Either he was

16

naturally surly, or he'd taken such an instant dislike to her, he wasn't prepared to accept her thanks. But in the silence her thoughts turned to where he was taking her. She assumed he had a home somewhere around—or was he taking her to a town? In her curiosity, tinged with anxiety, she revised her decision not to speak until spoken to.

"Er, where are we going?" she asked hesitantly, fearing a rebuff.

"Home!" He said the word with a possessiveness that sent a little quiver down her spine. He hadn't said "my home," or "my house." Just the one word, as if he were talking to someone who was on intimate terms with him rather than to a stranger.

"How far is it now?" She realized suddenly that she liked the sound of his voice, even when he spoke impatiently. The tones were deeply masculine, quick and sure, as if he knew exactly what he was about and never needed to hesitate.

"A couple of miles," he responded. Janna could hear rather than see that he was amused for some reason, and her impression was confirmed by his next words. "Relax. You're far safer with me than you were back there."

She flushed with embarrassment at his insinuating tone and was glad it was dark enough that he couldn't see her reaction. But his amusement was better than his impatience.

"What's your name?" The stranger sounded relaxed now, but Janna didn't know whether his relaxation was a result of his amusement at her worries or if he was glad they were nearing their destination.

"Janna." His casual question brought a momentary stab of remembrance. If Frank hadn't broken their engagement to marry Mellie, Janna would be Mrs. Frank Fairchild now. With a touch of defiance, she supplied the rest of her name. "Janna Wilding." After all, it was a perfectly good name. Shrugging off her brief excursion into the past, she looked at him with curiosity. "What's yours?"

"Cal Burke." And then as the dark bulk of a house became visible ahead through the blowing snow, he continued on a satisfied note. "We're here." And he pulled into a lane leading to the house.

"I'm sorry if I'll be putting your family to any trouble?" Janna half asked and half apologized. "Do you have room for me?"

His short laugh disconcerted her. "No trouble," he drawled, the amusement back in his voice. "I live alone. There's plenty of room."

As the house was obviously quite large, Janna didn't doubt that there would be room for her, but for the moment, she was concentrating more on the fact that she would be alone with him in it—for how long?

"No comment?" Cal had pulled to a stop and was eyeing her with intent appraisal, although she didn't think he could see much in the dim light. He turned off the key and sat a moment, waiting for her to reply.

"No, why should there be?" Janna swallowed nervously. "I'm very grateful you're taking me in." She knew her voice had betrayed the nervousness she felt when Cal Burke chuckled. But he didn't comment. Instead, he opened the door and swung his long legs out the opening. She had her own door open when he came around to help her out, and he kept his arm around her waist as they crossed the snow-covered ground to the house. Janna tried to concentrate on her footing and ignore the effect of his

18

nearness, but it was hard when he exuded such powerful masculinity. She was relieved when they finally climbed the steps to the house and he let her go to open the door.

He preceded her into a hallway and switched on a light, and as Janna followed him in, he swept off his hat with one hand and reached behind her to close the door with the other. The action brought him very close to her, and for the first time Janna was able to see his face clearly. Her eyes widened in astonishment. He was incredibly good-looking!

Black, thickly waving hair framed a tanned face with hard, purposeful features that were just saved from utter ruthlessness by a firm, but somehow sensitive—and disturbingly sensual—mouth. She was staring at that mouth when she became aware that his lips had twisted into a crooked line of amusement. Raising startled eyes to his, she found herself staring into two of the clearest, bluest eyes she'd ever seen, and she flushed with embarrassment at the knowing, slightly cynical expression contained there. What must he think of her standing there staring at him for what must have been a full minute?

Trying to dispel any notion she might have given him that she was attracted by his appearance, Janna turned quickly away from him and moved farther into the hallway.

"In here." Cal passed her and went into a room on his left, pausing to switch on a lamp just inside the door, then walking to a large fireplace on one wall. "I'll have to make a fire," he said, "but looks like I'll have to go out and get some wood first." He indicated a sofa in front of the fireplace. "Sit down while I turn up the heat and get the wood. Sorry, it's so cold in here, but I've been away." His blue eyes flicked over her briefly, dispassionately, as he

19

turned to leave the room, and Janna merely nodded at him as she settled onto the sofa he'd indicated.

When he'd gone, she studied the room with interest, liking what she saw. Incredibly, there was a white bear skin rug between the sofa and the empty fieldstone fireplace. She could hardly believe it. All of her life she'd heard about them, but this was the first time she'd actually seen one. She couldn't resist stooping to rub the hairy head and then gave a little self-conscious laugh of amusement at her action.

The sofa was patterned in vivid yellows, browns, and oranges, and there were scattered chairs around which picked up those tones in solid colors. One wall was taken up with bookshelves, and the volumes resting there looked well-thumbed. Janna would have liked to see what Cal's taste in reading was like but decided against an exploration at the moment.

The third wall was taken up with a large picture window, beside which hung a magnificent Indian tapestry depicting a hunting scene. Under the tapestry was a mahogany table that gleamed with polish. The floor was carpeted in a neutral brown except around the edges of the room and in front of the fireplace where a hardwood floor shone in the soft lighting.

All in all it was a pleasant, tastefully decorated room where one could relax and enjoy a warm fire, a good book, and the feeling of being secure against the wild weather outside. At least it would be warm when Cal got back with the firewood.

Shivering against the cold, Janna huddled on the sofa to wait. It was some time before a slight noise made her look up. Cal was standing in the doorway, his arms loaded with wood, and he was watching her. But even as she raised her head, he was moving toward the fireplace where he dumped the wood and began to make up a fire quickly and competently.

Janna studied the back of his head, wondering if she'd imagined that he'd been watching her. And if he had, what difference did it make? He was probably just as curious about her as she was about him. He probably didn't have to rescue women everyday of the week, although she thought it very probable that most women would give their eye teeth to be rescued by such a man. He was undeniably attractive. In fact, it was just as well she wasn't heartwhole herself right now in these intimate circumstances. At least her disastrous engagement to Frank was good for something.

"How old are you?" He spoke so abruptly that Janna jumped slightly.

"Er, twenty-five." He turned his head to look at her, his eyebrows lifted in surprise, and Janna frowned. That was the general reaction she got when she revealed her age. She looked seventeen at the most, and it always irritated her when someone made the inevitable observation about it. But surprisingly, Cal didn't. He just looked at her consideringly, then turned back to the fire. After a moment, he spoke again.

"I'm thirty-five." Janna had been wondering, but not for the world had she considered asking. "Sooner or later every woman I meet asks me that question. I thought I'd save time and satisfy both our curiosities."

Janna stirred impatiently. The arrogance of the man! What made him think she cared? But then she remembered uncomfortably that she'd certainly stared at him long enough earlier to make him assume she might. She made up her mind right then to treat him with cool politeness in case he was under the impression she was interested in him. He was most likely swamped with female adulation and always had been. But she wasn't going to fall under his spell, and he'd better learn that right off.

A shiver of reaction hit her as she felt a wave of warmth from the fireplace. The blaze had caught, and the logs were crackling fiercely. To her embarrassment, once the shivers started, she couldn't make them stop, and tremor after tremor shook her body.

"Come over here and sit by the fire," he ordered in his high-handed way. But Janna didn't want to argue with him right now. The fire looked heavenly. She moved at once to sit on the ledge surrounding the fireplace and then held out her hands to the blaze, trying to control her shivers and grateful beyond words that she had a fire to sit by instead of still being out in the cold of her car. She could hear the wind howling outside the window, and she hated to think what the temperature must be down to now.

"Would you like some coffee?" Cal was standing beside her watching her expressive face reflect her thoughts. His smile seemed genuine, without the cynical overtones that put her back up.

"Yes, please." She looked at him gratefully and tried not to sound as hungry as she felt. But he seemed to guess.

"I might as well fix something to eat as well," he said, as he moved to the door. "Bacon and eggs all right?"

Janna was torn between being a polite guest and the hunger in her stomach. Her stomach won. "It sounds marvelous," she admitted, and he smiled at her again—a charming, devastating smile—and turned away. "Can I help?" she remembered to call after him, but he shook his head.

"I can manage." And then he was gone.

Janna tried to close her mind to the effect his smile had had on her and settled back to wait again. The heat from the fire began to make her feel drowsy, and as she was warmer now, she stood to remove her coat. She was wearing a pair of jeans and a white, turtle-necked sweater, both of which set off her figure to good effect, but her own appearance was the farthest thing from her mind right now. She was more concerned about her reactions to one Cal Burke and how she was going to hide them from him. Indeed, she wondered how it was that she could allow him to affect her at all. Was she so shallow that she could forget Frank at the first occasion that she came into contact with another attractive man? A man she'd probably never see again once the storm let up enough that she could continue to travel?

She wished heartily that she weren't going to be stuck here alone with him for very long. He was entirely too masculine and virile to leave her unmoved by his presence, but somehow she had to keep their relationship casual. She didn't want to be another in what she was sure was a long line of female admirers. And under the present intimate circumstances, it would be all too easy for him to take advantage of the situation.

She was mulling over these thoughts when she heard him returning, and she swung around to find him just entering the room.

"The food's ready if you are," he said easily.

"Thank you." She gave him an uncertain smile. "I'm starved."

Cal didn't turn away as she crossed the room to join him. His startling blue eyes traveled the full length of her body, taking an inventory that made Janna burn with embarrassment. She'd never been so thoroughly appraised by a man, and she crossed her arms to hug her slim waist, trying to give the impression she was still cold.

At her movement Cal quirked his mouth in an ironic smile. "You shouldn't be so self-conscious, Janna," he drawled, using her name as if they'd known each other for years instead of less than an hour. "With a figure like yours, there's no need to hide it." Flicking the blue lightning of his glance over her again, lingering for a moment on the pink of her cheeks, he stepped back and allowed her to precede him into the hall.

Janna thought it best to ignore his comment on her figure. She knew she wasn't bad to look at. In fact, she'd had enough interest from the opposite sex to confirm her father's assertion that she was "better than pretty." But somehow Cal's way of affirming the fact created a breathless confusion in her that was totally unlike her usual reaction to compliments.

"Through here." Cal was reaching around her to open a door, and the movement brought him close to her. In fact, he actually took her arm as he ushered her into a yellow-and-white kitchen where the smell of bacon and coffee made her mouth water in anticipation. But her hunger wasn't enough to take her mind off the feel of his hand on her arm. The sensation burned her skin even through the cloth of her sweater. She was debating how to pull away from him, when he dropped his hold of his own accord.

"Sit down, Janna," he invited, and she obeyed willingly, taking in the fact that he'd gone to the trouble of setting two neat place settings and that the food on the table looked as if it had been cooked by an expert. Cal Burke

24

was a surprising man in more ways than one, she thought rather uncomfortably, as he seated himself opposite her.

Cal reached over and filled her cup with coffee, and Janna raised it to her lips gratefully. It had been hours since she'd had anything to eat or drink, and she dug into the food with relish, even forgetting about the disturbing man across from her in the enjoyment of the food. It was only after she'd had two helpings of everything and three cups of coffee that she noticed Cal had barely touched his own food. Instead, he was lounging back in his chair and watching her eat with an amused smile on his sensuous mouth.

Janna stopped chewing in the middle of a bite, momentarily self-conscious under his scrutiny and embarrassingly aware that she'd been making a pig out of herself. She swallowed the half-chewed bite in a gulp.

"Aren't you hungry?" she asked tentatively, noting that she hadn't left much to satisfy his hunger if he were.

"I had a late dinner," he said, and now his blue eyes were shining with suppressed laughter.

Janna's appetite had deserted her completely now, but she finished what was left on her plate and accepted another cup of coffee. "Thank you. That was delicious."

"I'm glad you enjoyed it," he nodded his head at her, but the humor was still evident in his eyes, and Janna was beginning to get a little irritated. All right, so she'd been hungry. But surely it wasn't as amusing as all that!

"It's amazing you stay so slender if you eat like that all the time," he persisted, and Janna's temper rose. Did he want her to apologize for eating his food? He'd fixed it for her, hadn't he? And he wasn't hungry, was he? A terrible suspicion hit her all at once. Had he been hungry, but let her eat his share too?

25

Janna looked at the all but empty dishes on the table and stuttered out the question. "Did . . . did I eat your share of the food as well as my own?" She looked at him with mortification written on her face, sure now that that was exactly what she'd done—and he had let her. "Oh, I'm sorry . . . I didn't realize." Her distress was evident.

"Forget it." He sounded completely unconcerned. "I told you I had a late meal. I only fixed this in the first place because you looked as if a puff of wind would blow you away."

Janna looked at him uncertainly, only half-convinced that he was telling the truth. "Well, it was very good," she said apologetically, and he laughed. The attractive sound of it and the change it wrought in his hard features had Janna staring at him again before she quickly caught herself up. This man was entirely too appealing for his own good—or for hers.

He pushed his chair back and stood up, and Janna did the same, gathering up her dishes to take them to the sink. "I'll wash these," she said a little breathlessly, trying to appear composed when she didn't feel it at all.

"Leave them for the morning," he said casually, but there was no mistaking the intent look he was giving her. He had noticed her confusion, and Janna hoped he thought it was still due to her embarrassment over eating his food. "It's time you were in bed."

His words threw her into even more confusion, and she saw his eyes gleam with interest as she rattled the dishes while placing them in the sink. What was the matter with her, Janna chastised herself angrily. She was behaving like a teen-ager! Of course, they had to go to bed. She glanced at her watch. It was three o'clock in the morning!

26

She licked her suddenly dry lips and turned to face him. "All right. I'll clean up in here when I get up."

He nodded his head sardonically and stood back to let her pass him. But as she drew even with him, he reached out and grabbed her arm lightly, causing her to jerk away instinctively. His eyes danced mischievously, but he didn't let go of her. "Relax, Janna," he drawled, as she stood stiffly, her eyes wide with apprehension. "There's a rule out here that you don't rescue a girl and then turn around and . . . er, force your attentions on her."

He let go of her then, and Janna felt like an immature child in the face of his comment. "I didn't . . ." She started to say she hadn't suspected him of anything untoward, but he cut her short.

"Didn't you?" There was a light challenge in his voice, but he moved past her to go to the door. "Sorry. I must have been mistaken when I thought I detected the beginnings of outraged maidenly virtue."

Janna followed him into the hallway, and he stopped in front of a closed door. "I'll put you into the room where my niece stays while she's here. That should make you feel secure."

Janna understood what he meant when he threw open the door and she saw the pink-and-white femininity of a very young girl's room displayed in front of her. He was telling her in no uncertain terms that he regarded her on a par with the child who normally occupied that room, and Janna felt unaccountably irritated. She wanted to protest that she was an adult, but she was afraid he would take it as an invitation to treat her as one in ways she wouldn't be able to handle.

"It's charming," she said as naturally as she could as she moved past him to enter the room. "Thank you and

. . . good night." She flashed him a defiant look that brought back the amusement to his eyes.

He nodded his head. "Good night, Janna," he drawled, and shut the door in her face!

Oh! Janna picked up a stuffed animal and threw it across the room. She didn't know if she were angry at herself or at him. She just knew she felt disturbed at the byplay that had just taken place. Why did she allow him to upset her like that? He was just another man, after all. More attractive than most, true. But she'd met many attractive men in the past and had even been pursued by them. And she'd managed to retain her virginity in spite of it. But Cal was treating her as if she were a complete innocent, and for some reason, it rankled. In fact, he had her completely confused. Did she want him to treat her as a woman or as a child?

Unable to answer the question in her own mind, she went into the adjoining bathroom to wash up for the night. By the time she came back into the bedroom, she'd cooled down enough to look forward to climbing into the pristine little bed with its pink-and-white checked spread. It was only after she'd shed all her clothes that she realized Cal hadn't brought in her bags and she had no nightgown. She debated about sleeping in her clothes—she certainly wasn't going to look him up and ask him to go out into the fury of the storm to get her bags—but she couldn't face putting the wrinkled, soiled garments on again. Shrugging, she climbed naked between the sheets, reflecting that Cal wasn't likely to come into her room uninvited—not after he'd gone to such pains to let her know how she appeared to him.

She snuggled down, shivering a little at the coolness of the sheets against her bare skin, but soon she was wrapped

28

in a heavenly cocoon of soft warmth. She was just dropping off to sleep when she heard the door open, and in the next instant the room was flooded with light.

Janna sat up unthinkingly, blinking her eyes rapidly when she saw Cal standing in the doorway, her bag in his hand. He dropped the bag to the floor, making no attempt to conceal his interest as Janna frantically pulled the covers up to her chin. They'd slipped down when she'd sat up, and she wasn't sure how much he'd been able to see before she recovered presence of mind enough to pull them up. But she was very much afraid he'd seen enough to know she had nothing on. His next words confirmed this.

"I thought you'd need this," he said softly and musingly, his eyes raking her form under the covers. "But I see you sleep in the raw . . . like me." He smiled mockingly as Janna blushed and shook her head negatively.

Her heart was beating so hard, she thought he must be able to hear it. He still had on his trousers, but had removed his shirt, and the sight of his brown, muscular shoulders and the dark hair on his chest, coupled with her awareness of her own vulnerable position, made their enforced intimacy almost unbearable.

"Thank . . ." Janna stopped and swallowed hard. "Thank you." She got the words out but was dismayed at the huskiness of her voice. She knew it was the result of having been almost asleep, but would he know that?

Her eyes widened with apprehension and she pushed back against the bed in a motion of withdrawal as Cal took a step into the room. Seeing this, he frowned thoughtfully and stopped. "Where would you like me to put it?" he asked, indicating the bag on the floor—and his own voice was huskier than she remembered it being only seconds

29

before. His eyes had darkened and were still taking all of her in, and Janna moved nervously under his stare.

"Oh, leave it there . . . please. Thank you again." She was rushing the words, she knew, but she wanted him to go. In the back of her mind, there was the traitorous thought that she wanted him to go because he disturbed her in a way that could prove highly dangerous if he made any attempt to impose his will. Could she stop him if he did? Would she want to?

She told herself she was relieved when he smiled mockingly again and turned to leave the room. He paused with one hand on the doorknob and gave her one last long look, and a tingling sensation went down Janna's spine.

"Good night," she faltered.

"Good night, Janna . . . and pleasant dreams," and he was gone.

Janna sighed and relaxed back against the pillows. She frowned impatiently at the tremor that went through her in remembering the way the sight of his body had affected her. Good heavens, was she as susceptible as all that? If so, it was going to be a very uncomfortable few days—or however long it took for this storm to pass.

A sudden thought had her scrambling from the bed to go to the door to lock it. But there was no lock. So she had to content herself with pulling a nightgown from her bag. She didn't know who she mistrusted more—Cal Burke or herself. But she felt some sense of security once she'd pulled the gown over her head. Not that it was much better than being nude, she thought ruefully as she caught sight of herself in the dresser mirror. The pale pink diaphanous material seemed to reveal more than it concealed. But at least it was a covering of some kind.

Janna snapped off the bedside light and climbed back

between the sheets, only to lie wakeful for some time with visions of Cal Burke's disturbing face and exciting body keeping her from sleep. But at last, her tired body succumbed to exhaustion and she drifted into a peaceful slumber. And if her dreams were filled with images of a dark face and two gleaming blue eyes, at least she was able to blame it on her subconscious. Wasn't she?

CHAPTER TWO

The howling of the wind outside the window woke Janna to a gray light filtering through the curtains. She knew where she was instantly, which was not surprising in view of the nature of her dreams all through the night. Frowning in perplexity, Janna wondered if it were just that she was more lonely than she'd realized, or if she would have reacted to Cal Burke so strongly regardless of her broken engagement and subsequent self-inflicted abstention from the company of men. It was a dangerous thought, and Janna determined that she'd have to be very careful while she was here. She didn't want to give Cal any sign of the feelings he aroused in her, nor did she want to acknowledge them to herself. She couldn't imagine anything more useless than encouraging a relationship that at best would amuse him, and at worst would leave her even more heartsore than she was already.

So deciding, she flung the covers aside, jumped out of bed, and scurried to the bathroom to escape the chill that hit her once out from under the warmth of the blankets. Back in the bedroom a few moments later, she was bending over her bag to get out some clean clothing when the door swung open, and Cal Burke confronted her. He was fully dressed, and stood watching calmly as Janna hastily searched for a robe. But it was in another bag, still in the trunk of her car.

"So you're up," he observed unnecessarily, and he leaned against the door jamb, his arms crossed over his chest, and let his eyes burn through the sheer material of Janna's nightgown where it clung to her slim hips and the rounded curves of her breasts. "Get cold, did you?" His nod indicated the silky pink gown, but the quirk of his mouth indicated he knew very well why she'd put it on, and that it had nothing to do with being cold.

And suddenly, Janna was angry. How dare he come into her room without even knocking and stand there inspecting her as if he had every right in the world to do so? Her brown eyes shot sparks as she straightened her shoulders and stared back at him, refusing to cower in the face of his appraisal.

"Don't you ever knock?" she said sharply, uncaring of the ungracious tone she used when she was a guest in his home. In her opinion his own manners left a lot to be desired.

A glint of frost touched the blue of his eyes, and one black eyebrow rose in arrogant disapproval. "This is my home. Why should I? I don't believe in locked doors . . . nor in false modesty." He swept her body with a glance that had hardened perceptibly. "I came to tell you break-fast will be ready in ten minutes." He straightened and turned to leave, but not before delivering a parting shot. "Don't bother to knock before entering the kitchen—I won't hold it against you."

Janna's anger was slow to die as she pulled on dark brown pants and a beige sweater that set off her curves and the coloring of her streaked, honey-beige hair. She jerked a comb through the long strands, fuming to herself at Cal

Burke's arrogance, his bad manners, and his conceit. But as a particularly heavy gust of wind shook the house, she reflected that if it hadn't been for him, she would most likely still be out in the blizzard raging outside—if she hadn't already frozen to death. The thought sobered her and cooled her anger.

Crossing to the window, she looked out to see snow piled in huge drifts while the air was still thick with it coming down to add even more to that already on the ground. The wind was blowing with such strength that it pushed the trees into wildly gesticulating positions as it blew snow into almost a horizontal line. She'd never seen anything to rival the sheer power of the storm that held her prisoner in Cal Burke's home. And it didn't look anywhere near abating, so that travel was out of the question.

The thought of traveling brought to mind the fact that she wouldn't be able to report to her new job on time. But if Cal would let her telephone, she could at least explain the circumstances and let her employers know she would be there as soon as the roads were cleared.

She went back to the dresser to apply a light coating of makeup, noting that her eyes reflected the anxiety she felt at being cooped up here alone with Cal Burke while her new job went waiting for lack of her presence. Fate was not being very kind to her lately, she thought wryly, as she put on a light layer of foundation and a pale coating of pink lipstick. But she would just have to make the best of it.

With a slight feeling of perturbation, she left her room to join Cal in the kitchen. The dishes they'd used the night before were missing, and she felt a little guilty at the realization that he'd washed them himself. The aroma of coffee filled the room, and she longed for a cup to strength-en her defenses against the man who stood at the stove stirring something in a pot. Janna thought she'd never seen a man look so thoroughly masculine while engaged in what was commonly termed woman's work.

"Sit down." Cal turned his remarkable blue eyes on her at last and flicked her up and down briefly, but thorough-ly. "This will be ready in a minute."

Janna seated herself at the table and studied him covert-ly from beneath her long black lashes. He had on jeans and a pale blue sweater that made his eyes seem even more intensely blue than they normally were. He held the long, lean length of his body with unstudied grace and power that spelled "male" in every inch. Janna dropped her gaze as he crossed to her and set the pot on a hot plate, then went back for the coffee.

"Do you like oatmeal?" His glance was cool, and his tone more so. Janna supposed he was still annoyed with her, but she wasn't about to apologize for her earlier re-mark about his failure to knock before entering her room. She considered she was within her rights to expect that courtesy.

"Yes, thank you," she replied, keeping her own voice cool to match his tone. She brushed aside the regret she felt at the strained atmosphere. It was probably a good thing it had developed, she thought cynically. And while it might not be pleasant, it was at least safer.

They ate in silence for a while before Janna brought up the subject of the telephone. "Would you mind if I put in a long-distance call to my employers . . . and to my fam-ily?" She sounded stiff, hating to ask for more favors from this man when he was already doing so much, and when they were not even on friendly terms. "I need to let my

35

family know I'm all right, and my employers need to be notified that I won't be reporting for work tomorrow."

"You're welcome to call anyone you like," he said coolly. "If the phone's in working order, that is."

Janna jerked her head up at this. "What do you mean?" And then as realization dawned, "Oh, the storm . . ." She bit her lip in consternation. She hadn't thought of the possibility that the storm would wreck communications. Somehow, it made their isolation seem even more intimate.

"Yes, the storm," he mocked her. "You're welcome to try, though. It's over there." He gestured to a yellow wall phone near the door.

"Excuse me." Janna couldn't wait to find out if her fears were justified, and she crossed to the telephone with trepidation. Her heart sank as the lack of a dial tone made it all too clear that the phone was dead. She jiggled the receiver a few times in the vain hope that she might be wrong. But it was useless, and finally she replaced the receiver and returned to the table, her shoulders drooping in unconscious dejection.

"It's dead, then?" Cal seemed unconcerned.

"Yes," Janna sighed.

Shrugging, Cal returned to eating, and resentment flared in Janna at his lack of understanding. How could she bear to be trapped in this house with him, having to fight her own attraction to him as well as his uncaring attitude? As she gazed around the room in an effort to keep her eyes off him, the answer presented itself. Work . . . If he'd let her, she could keep herself so busy around this house, she wouldn't have the time or the energy to worry about him during the day and she'd be too tired at night to dream.

Clearing her throat nervously, she waited to catch his eyes before voicing her suggestion. "Mr. Burke?"

He broke in abruptly. "Cal." He corrected her firmly, as if determined she wasn't going to be allowed the barrier of formality between them.

"Cal, then," she spoke awkwardly, annoyed at this insistence that she call him by his first name, but at some level of her awareness, she knew that she was traitorously pleased. "I'd like to earn my keep while I'm here. I mean, I can't just eat your food and sit around doing nothing . . ." Her voice trailed off as he leaned back in his chair, pinioning her with an enigmatic blue gleam.

"What'd you have in mind?" His voice was soft and huskily suggestive.

Janna caught her breath at the insinuation in his question and in his tone. "Housework . . . the cooking . . . things like that." Her voice quavered, and she lowered her eyes to escape his.

"It's the 'things like that' that interest me," he murmured, leaning forward as she glanced up nervously.

"I don't know what you mean," she parried, swallowing convulsively. She was unable to wrench her gaze from the ruthless sensuousness of his hard mouth, try as she might.

"Don't you?" He smiled inimically, and Janna finally found the strength to tear her eyes away from his face.

"No, I don't!" Janna was determined not to encourage him in whatever game he was playing with her, but her pulses were racing just the same.

He shrugged then, and a look of skepticism replaced the interest on his face. "Well, perhaps not," he drawled cynically. "Although I would have thought anyone your age wouldn't be quite so naive."

Janna just kept herself from gasping out loud in indignation. Had he seriously thought she would be willing to enter into that kind of an arrangement with him? He must have been more successful with women than she'd imagined—and he didn't seem to have a very high opinion of them at that!

"If you want to work around here, suit yourself. I suppose it'll give you something to keep your . . . er, nerves steady." Cal sounded bored and disinterested now, and Janna flashed him a look of irritation, whereupon he mocked her again. "These storms have a way of inducing cabin fever if you're not used to them."

Janna decided to accept his words at face value. Anything to get off this dangerous subject. "How long do you think the storm will last?" she inquired casually, hoping the outlook was good. She was doomed to disappointment.

"Could be a couple of days—could be a week," Cal replied.

"That long?" Janna couldn't conceal her dismay. Would they hold the job for her? And would her nerves stand the enforced intimacy with Cal that long?

Cal was watching her with a calculating expression on his handsome features. "What's the matter? Worried about your job, or . . ." he paused and swept her up and down with a bold glance. "Worried about the proprieties of the situation?"

"Both!" Janna answered him before she thought, and then regretted it instantly as a derisive gleam entered the electric blue eyes.

"Well, I can relieve your mind on one point. I'm not in the habit of seducing virgins—and you are one, aren't you?" Cal ignored her gasp of outrage. "And I would have thought if you're any good at whatever it is you do, they'd

38

hold your job for you." He stood up and went to lean his back against the counter, finishing the coffee in his cup and setting it down. "What do you do anyway?"

"I'm a certified public accountant," she snapped, anger still simmering at his cool assumption that she was an innocent, and that he could seduce her whether she were or not. How did he know anyway, she wondered.

"And I am good at it," she added for good measure. "It's just that . . . well, the job's at a coal mine, and they didn't want to hire a woman in the first place, so . . ."

"A mine!" Cal's eyes narrowed and a line of disapproval marked his brow. "Why in the hell would you want to work at a coal mine?" He didn't give her a chance to answer him. "They were right not to want to hire you. And if they're smart, they'll withdraw their offer!"

Janna jumped up from her chair and faced him angrily. Nothing annoyed her more than the prejudice of an arrogant male when faced with what he considered the invasion of his territory by a mere female.

"And why shouldn't I work at a coal mine?" she flared at him. "I have the experience and the qualifications, and I want to do it!"

Cal looked her up and down expressively. "And you're a woman in case you haven't noticed," he said coldly. "A coal mine is no place for a woman!" He paused, and then continued, a jeering note entering his voice. "Unless she's looking for a man?"

The slight note of disgust in his tone raised Janna's temper a few degrees higher, but she closed her mouth firmly. What was the use of trying to change an ingrained prejudice like this? She'd tried it before with other men, arguing until she was blue in the face. The only thing that

39

ever convinced them was competent action, and she wasn't in a position to convince Cal Burke of the quality of her work—nor that she wasn't in the least interested in the men working at the coal mine.

"Oh, forget it!" She turned sharply away from him and began to gather up the breakfast dishes.

To her surprise, he chuckled. "Giving up so soon?" he inquired mockingly. "I thought you'd fight to the bitter end defending your rights."

Janna glared at him. "I've learned it's a waste of time to defend anything against a closed mind," she said huffily, and carried the dishes to the sink. She bent to search in the compartment under the sink for some soap and couldn't find any. "Where's the soap?" she said shortly, uncaring that she was behaving rudely to this man who'd saved her life.

Cal didn't answer her. He simply reached in and brought out the soap from where it had been resting in plain sight. Janna had been so angry, she hadn't seen it.

"Thank you," she said sarcastically.

"You're welcome," he said exaggeratedly, bowing his dark head in a parody of courtesy and laughing at her silently all the while.

Janna concentrated on running hot water and slinging dishes into the sink with dangerous abandon.

"Careful," Cal murmured. "I've been known to fire household help when they cause more damage than they cure."

Janna gave him an expressive look and began to handle the dishes with exaggerated care. She would have loved to fling a handful of soap suds into his mocking devil's face.

"That's better," he said gravely, taking note of her lessened violence as if he didn't know she was silently defying him. "Keep that up, and you may earn yourself a new job—you'd be imminently more suited to housekeeping, hmmm?" And with a laugh he moved away toward the door.

Janna clenched her teeth to keep from flinging a retort at him, and he paused before going out.

"I'll be in my study if you need me," he said matter-of-factly. "It's the third door on the right down the hall."

Janna waited just long enough to make sure he was gone before she swung around and pitched a handful of soap bubbles at the empty place where he'd stood. She felt like a coward for not having done it while he was there to receive the brunt of it, but down deep, she was afraid of what the consequences would have been. Cal Burke was undoubtedly capable of anything.

She worked off her anger by banging around in the kitchen, all the while thinking furious thoughts and punctuating them with slammed cabinet doors. After finishing the dishes, she found a broom and a mop and before long, she had the kitchen shining, with her own good humor restored as a bonus. She put away the cleaning supplies and switched on the coffeemaker, deciding it was time to put her feet up before finding something else to do.

But instead of sitting down, she wandered to the kitchen window to watch the storm still raging outside. It hadn't slackened at all as far as she could determine. If anything, it looked worse than before. As she turned away, she noticed a small radio on a shelf and switched it on to check the weather forecast. For the moment, she found nothing but music, so she left it on a clear station that specialized in country western music and checked the coffee. It wasn't quite ready yet, so she wandered around the room, noting again how cheerful and cozy it was. She wondered who

41

kept house for Cal and decided she pitied whoever it was. The man probably paid low wages and stood over his help with a whip.

She chuckled to herself at the picture of Cal Burke as a latter day Simon Legree and then sobered as she heard the voice of a newscaster on the radio.

> Wyoming and several surrounding states are undergoing the worst winter storm of the last ten years. Major highways are closed, and we have reports of the deaths of several motorists stranded in their cars. More news after this word from our sponsor.

Janna stood pale and thoughtful, aware as she hadn't been before of just how much she owed to Cal Burke. She might not like him particularly, but he had saved her life—there was no doubt of that now. She felt uncomfortably ashamed of her behavior toward him, even though a small corner of her mind protested that she'd had provocation. But the justification seemed pitiful when her mind conjured up a picture of herself frozen and lifeless in the confines of her car on that lonely highway.

Coming to a decision, she moved to take two cups and saucers from the cabinet. It wasn't too late to show her gratitude, and she intended to do just that. No more arguments. She'd help as much as she could around the house and try to be as inconspicuous a guest as possible. And to begin with, she'd make her peace with her host.

Moments later, Janna stood with a tray of coffee in her hands outside the door of what she hoped was Cal's study. She knocked gingerly, and receiving no reply, she knocked louder.

"Come in!" Cal sounded abstracted and impatient, and his face reflected that mood when Janna came through the door. He sat at a large wooden desk with papers strewn around him, and he was frowning with concentration as he studied a document in his hand. It was obvious he didn't approve of the contents. He muttered a muffled "damn!" and then raised his head to see Janna standing hesitantly just inside the door with the tray of coffee in her hands. He put down the paper and smiled at her ruefully.

"I thought you might like some coffee." Janna felt almost meek in his presence until she saw the sudden appraising light in his eyes. Surely he didn't think she was finding excuses to be with him, she thought indignantly.

"That would be nice," he answered quietly, as he stood up and came around the desk to sit on the edge, staring at her in that curiously intent way that made her so uncomfortable. She wished he wouldn't always concentrate quite so forcefully on whatever held his attention . . . in this case, herself.

"Where would you like it?" She retained her outward composure, but the sight of his superb body and the impact of his blue eyes were having their usual effect on her.

"Over here, I think," Cal said as he moved to a brown leather sofa in front of still another fireplace. This one was smaller than the one she'd seen the night before, and there was a cheerful blaze in it creating a warmth and intimacy that slowed Janna's steps as she walked to join Cal. She set the tray down on a table in front of the sofa.

"Do you mind if I join you?" Her brown eyes darted a nervous look at him as he stood on the other side of the table.

"I was hoping you would," he responded softly, and against her will, Janna looked into the mesmerizing blue

43

of his eyes, only managing to drag her own away through sheer determination to keep her distance. Why did he have to be quite so attractive, she thought forlornly. Why couldn't I have been rescued by a fat pig farmer with a wife and ten kids?

"I . . . er . . . I wanted to talk to you," she stammered out, feeling as gawky as a girl on her first date as she sat down to pour the coffee. To her dismay, he sat down only inches away from her. She'd hoped he would occupy one of the chairs a safe distance away. Her hand shook as she raised the coffeepot to pour, and she left his cup on the tray rather than risk him seeing how nervous she was.

"Talk away," he murmured, a thread of amusement in his voice as he reached to pick up his cup. Janna noted that his own hand was rock steady, and it annoyed her unreasonably.

"I want to apologize," she said in a rush, determined to stick to her purpose. His eyebrows were raised in polite inquiry. "For arguing with you . . . and, er, snapping at you this morning." He wasn't helping a bit, she thought miserably as he watched her, saying nothing. Sighing in resignation, she continued. "I owe you my life, Mr. Burke . . ."

"Cal," he prompted once again, an underlying note of firmness beneath the cool politeness in his voice.

"Cal," Janna acknowledged. "Anyway, I heard on the radio that several people died in their cars last night, and if you hadn't found me . . ." She shuddered expressively and Cal broke in.

"I told you to forget it," he said roughly. "Anyone would have done the same."

"But it wasn't anyone," Janna protested. "It was you.

And I've been behaving abominably to you when I should have been . . ."

"Oh, hell!" Cal shifted his weight impatiently, bringing his thigh just that much closer to Janna's. "Save me from the gratitude of a woman. Maybe when I'm eighty years old, I'll need it. Right now, I don't!"

Janna moved her shoulders slightly, hurt at his attitude. "People need to express their gratitude, Mr. . . . Cal . . . And I only wanted you to know how I feel." She glanced up at him, a small frown creasing her forehead. "Wouldn't you want to say thank you if someone had saved your life?" She asked the question with some asperity, facing him squarely for the first time. Instantly, she knew it was a mistake. She was caught in the blue flame of two diabolically compelling blue eyes—eyes that took in her flushed cheeks and trembling mouth with sudden purpose.

"I think I'd be inclined to show my gratitude with action rather than words, Janna." His deep voice caressed her name, and suddenly every fiber of her body was awake and aware of him. She struggled to look away, but it was as if he held her pinned to him though he wasn't even touching her—not with anything but his eyes.

"I'll . . . I'll be happy to show my gratitude if you'll tell me how . . . what . . .?" Janna stopped, knowing how provocative her words were and just as aware that she'd meant them to be provocative. She must be going crazy to play with fire like this!

"Would you now?" A fire had lit all at once behind the blue eyes, and Cal moved closer to her, raising a hand to her chin and studying her intently. Janna drew back sluggishly, but it was only a token resistance, and Cal seemed to know it, for he pulled her to him abruptly and pressed

45

her back against the leather of the sofa. "Then I'll show you what I want, shall I, little refugee?" He murmured the words against her lips, and Janna's purely hypocritical no was smothered by the firmness of his mouth.

It was as if she'd never been kissed before. Not even Frank had stirred her blood like this. She felt Cal's hard body pressing against her, and it was useless to pretend that she didn't want to press back against him . . . in fact, it proved impossible to pretend anything. She simply reacted, opening her mouth to receive his kisses, moaning his name helplessly when he shifted them both down to lie side by side on the sofa, catching her breath when his hands moved over her to stir her responses to wildfire.

Never had she lost her head with a man—but now she couldn't help herself. She was scarcely aware of the control Cal exercised when she moved to pull him onto her, but she felt him shudder when she ran her hands over his back and down to his hips. She heard her own voice pleading with him as if in a dream.

"Cal . . . please, please . . . I want you so."

At her words, he sat up abruptly and then stood, moving to stand in front of the fireplace, leaving her with the ache of abandonment and unsatisfied desire—and then with the misery of humiliation. For a moment, she couldn't believe that she had behaved so recklessly—and that she owed her salvation from that recklessness to the man who stood with his back to her a few steps away. She sat up hastily and tried to stand on weakened legs. All she wanted was to get away from him and hide her humiliation in the safety of her room. His voice stopped her as he swung around upon hearing her movement.

"Are you a virgin, Janna?" His voice was clipped and cold, piercing her with what she thought was contempt.

46

"Yes!" The word was out of her mouth of its own accord as she looked at him with horrified shame, tears of mortification not far away. She stood and started for the door, but he took a step and caught her arm, swinging her around to face him.

"Well, don't make a federal case out of it," he said impatiently, but his hands were moving disturbingly on her arms as he held her. She knew she ought to pull away from him, but she found she couldn't. Even now her humiliation wasn't proving to be much of a defense against his attraction. "Like I said . . . we don't take advantage of our guests out here . . . not while they're under our roofs, anyway." He was mocking again, but this time the mockery seemed to be self-directed. "Even uninvited guests deserve that protection!"

Janna felt as if he'd slapped her! Now she did find the strength to pull away, but instead of running to the door, she bent with cold purposefulness to pick up the tray of coffee on the table. He wasn't to know from her actions how much he'd hurt her.

"I'm sorry, Janna," Cal rubbed his hand over the back of his head in frustration. "I didn't mean that the way it sounded."

"But it's true, isn't it," she said lifelessly. "I am an uninvited guest. And from now on, I'll stay out of your way—you don't have to worry about me making a nuisance of myself from here on out." She was halfway to the door when she heard his muffled, "Damn it, there's no need . . ." but she didn't stick around to let him finish. Once out of his study, she almost ran to the kitchen to get rid of the tray, and then she hurried to her bedroom to fling herself down on the pink-and-white bed and let the tears flow.

It was a long time before she was able to think coherently. But when she could, she formed her purpose with all the strength she was capable of in the face of Cal Burke's devastating appeal. She'd work in his house until she fairly dropped with fatigue . . . and she'd be polite when she had to be near him. She didn't intend for that to happen except perhaps at meals. But never again would she let him know that she was so susceptible to him that she would have given herself to him without thought for her principles . . . without thought for anything but the mind-dulling, physical attraction he could create in her at will. That she was still susceptible would be her secret and her cross to bear.

The decision enabled her to drag herself from the bed and wash her face and hands. Looking at her pale face in the mirror, she supposed she looked the same as she always had. It was a good thing faces didn't necessarily show the turmoil that could rage inside a person, she thought wryly. If they did, her own face would be cracked into a million pieces.

For the rest of the day, Cal stayed in his study, and Janna worked on the rest of the house as if her life depended on finding every mote of dust. She vacuumed everything in sight and cleaned every bathroom, until she was almost reeling with tiredness. Then she made dinner, and when it was almost ready, she went with reluctant steps to call Cal.

As she tapped on the study door, she felt ridiculously formal in view of the abandoned way she had behaved such a short time before. And this time he didn't call out for her to come in, but instead he threw open the door with a suddenness that made her step back. They stood looking

48

at one another for a moment, he with a tired frown, she with a tired stiffness, until Janna found her voice.

"Dinner's ready . . . if you're hungry." She lifted a hand wearily to push back a strand of honey-streaked hair that had fallen onto her smooth forehead and waited for him to reply.

Cal leaned his tall frame against the door, taking in the slump of her shoulders and the droop of her sensitive mouth. "For God's sake, what have you been doing to yourself?" He sounded wearily condemnatory, and Janna turned away to start back to the kitchen.

She wished now that she'd taken the trouble to have a shower and fix herself up a little before calling him, but the exhaustion deadened her feelings to the extent that she didn't really care all that much. What was the use in fixing herself up for him anyway?

She felt rather than heard him following her, and she answered his question somewhat after the fact. "Oh, I've been cleaning a little here and there," she said with an attempt at casualness, straightening her shoulders to try to conceal her fatigue. But her attempt at concealment came too late.

"Hmmm . . ." He sounded half-amused, half-irritated. "From the sound of that vacuum cleaner, I'd have said you cleaned more than a little."

Janna stopped just inside the kitchen and looked back at him, her eyes wide and startled. "Oh, did the noise disturb you? I'm sorry . . . I didn't think . . ." She was experiencing an irritation of her own at his lack of appreciation, along with chagrin at having disturbed his concentration.

"Oh, it's perfectly all right with me if you want to wear yourself out cleaning a perfectly clean house. My housekeeper was just here yesterday to get ready for my return."

Janna gazed at him in speechless indignation. Of all the gall! To have her efforts passed off in this fashion was the final straw in a long, tiring, thoroughly frustrating day! "Oh, you're insufferable!" She was sputtering in her anger. "You could have told me that this morning, instead of saying I could clean if I wanted to! Well, I hope your dinner chokes you, that's all I can say!"

She tried to push past him, intending to go to her room and nurse her grievances in solitude. She wasn't in the least hungry anyway, especially if she had to sit across from this . . . this monster!

He caught her and held her easily, struggle though she would, and at last, she collapsed into weak tears against the very shoulder she'd promised herself to avoid.

"Hold on, little snow orphan," he murmured against her ear, his voice sending delicious thrills down her spine even through her tears. "I didn't mean to send you off the deep end." He was rubbing her back with strong, gentle fingers, and in spite of herself she savored the feel of his hard body against her and the intoxicatingly clean smell of him so close to her. "I'm tired, too," he sighed finally and pushed her gently away from him, reaching into his pocket for a handkerchief.

She stood like a child while he wiped her eyes, but her emotions bore no resemblance to the uncomplicated innocence she remembered from her earlier days. Now they were a twisted jumble of uncertainty, anxiety . . . and desire. He could still rouse her as no man ever had, even through the layers of fatigue and emotional exhaustion that wrapped her round like a cloud.

50

"Come on," he said, turning her gently toward the kitchen. "Let's eat and then start over again, shall we?"

Janna moved with him, incapable of defying him—and if she were honest, she didn't want to be away from him. So they sat at the table together and ate the grilled steak, baked potatoes, and green salad she'd prepared. It wasn't long before Janna felt almost normal again, relaxing into a bemused acceptance of the fact that she was very close to losing her heart to this man who treated her with such bewildering contradictoriness—gentle one moment, cutting her to the quick the next. Only the realization that, just as with Frank, she was going to have to say good-bye to him soon, kept her from losing all control of her battered heart. But she didn't think she would be able to forget Cal Burke as quickly as she was losing the memory of Frank's image. Strangely, since meeting Cal, the pain that had been her constant companion for the last few weeks had dulled into an almost indetectable niggling at the back of her mind—brought out mostly to badger herself into resisting the attraction for the man seated across from her.

"What have you been doing to make you so tired?" Her question came out normally as she poured another cup of coffee for Cal. She was grateful for her seeming calmness and didn't question where it came from.

"I'm having my taxes audited in a couple of weeks," he answered her after a brief pause. "And it's amazing how hard it is to make sense of the notes and bills after they're a few months old." He smiled ruefully at her. "It's enough to make a lamb turn into a lion."

Janna's heart sang at his explanation. Was this his way of apologizing? She felt a rush of tenderness as she looked

51

at the lines of weariness etched into the hard lines of his face.

"Are you suggesting that you normally have the disposition of a lamb?" she teased and then smiled at the sardonic quirk of one black eyebrow. "Because I won't believe that. I'm afraid I see you more as a perpetual lion."

Cal relaxed back into his chair and looked at her, a gleam of mischief sparkling in the blue of his eyes. "And how do you see yourself, I wonder?" he drawled. "As a snow bunny? Or as a honey bear?" His eyes took in the color of her hair and the smooth curve of her cheek. "A honey bear, I think—with a lovely pelt and sharp little teeth!"

Janna gave him a quick glance from under her long eyelashes. "Of course," she parried. "We poor little bears need those sharp teeth to protect our skins from the hunters."

"And from the mountain lions?" He was enjoying their sparring, and it pleased Janna that she could bring him out of his tired mood like this, even if the direction their conversation was taking could prove dangerous to her equilibrium.

"Especially from the mountain lions," she agreed equitably. "That's the first thing mother bears teach their cubs. Beware the lions!"

Cal laughed softly. "But children don't always listen to their mothers, do they, Janna? They like to tempt fate on their own—and sometimes they get in trouble over their heads."

Janna shifted nervously. She didn't much like the way the conversation was going now. She didn't want to be told in so many words by this man that she was beating her head . . . and her heart . . . against a stone wall. She already knew it.

"If they're lucky, they survive . . . and they learn," she said quickly, briskly, willing him to drop the game she'd entered so carelessly. A change of subject was definitely in order.

"If you'd like, I can help you with your taxes." Her quick shift didn't go unnoticed, she knew, but Cal seemed willing to go along with it.

"How?" He sat up and replenished his coffee cup, his manner casual.

"I'm a CPA," she reminded him, and then bit her lip in vexation. Of course, he wouldn't take help from her, she thought sourly. She was a woman, after all. Cooking and cleaning were her provinces according to him. But he surprised her.

"All right." Janna looked at him, blinking in disorientation at his acceptance of her offer. "Not tonight—we've both had about all we can handle for one day," he continued—and was there a glimmer of mockery in his voice? "We'll get started tomorrow morning."

He shifted the subject on his own now, getting up to look through the curtains at the storm still raging outside. "Heard any more weather reports?" He seemed restless as he paced to the other window, looking for all the world like the lion she'd compared him to.

"No," Janna said, as she began to gather up the dishes. "Not since this morning." All she wanted now was her bed and the peace of oblivion. "They said then that the storm could last another day or so." She crossed to the sink and began to stack the dishes wearily, then ran hot water and started to wash them.

Cal came to stand beside her, looking critically at her

53

tired face. Somehow, she wasn't in the least surprised when he grabbed a tea towel and began to dry the dishes as she washed them. It seemed the most natural thing in the world to be standing beside him, sharing a mundane chore in silent companionship.

When they finished, she stretched her aching arms over her head in a long yawn, sleepily unaware that her action exposed the length of her lovely body to the alert blue eyes watching her, or that Cal's jaw tightened as the material of her sweater tautened over the firm swell of her breasts.

"Time for bed," he said abruptly, a grim note in his voice that made Janna wonder confusedly what she'd done to set him off this time.

"Fine with me," she said with resignation, tossing the length of her hair over her shoulder as she turned toward the door. She felt dimly unhappy at the change in Cal's mood, but she didn't want to examine too closely why his moods should affect her own so much. "Good night," she said sulkily, and she didn't look at him as she headed for the safety of her temporary bedroom.

"Janna . . ." Cal's voice was curiously strained, and Janna paused to look at him over her shoulder. He crossed to her and turned her to face him, his hands restlessly kneading her shoulders.

Janna's heart pounded at his touch, and she hoped he wasn't going to kiss her. She knew she didn't have the strength to resist him now any more than she'd been able to earlier.

But he only pushed the hair away from her face to tuck it behind her ears, and then rubbed his thumbs over the clean, firm line of her jaw. "Sleep well, Janna. I'll *knock* on your door to wake you in the morning." With a mocking smile at this reference to her earlier complaint, he turned her around to face the door and gave her a little push toward it.

Janna kept going, but she couldn't resist flashing a quick glance at him over her shoulder when she reached the door. He'd turned away and was standing at the window again. He looked vulnerable, and it was a peculiar sensation to see his straight, hard back and the dark hair curling on his neck projecting vulnerability. She left the room quickly before she could give in to the sudden, insane impulse to go to him and put her arms around his waist. He didn't need her comfort, she knew. It was an illusion, created by her own need to touch him again.

As she prepared for bed, Janna knew that she would have to fight such impulses constantly while she was here, and she reflected with some consternation that she was becoming a stranger to herself in the company of Cal Burke. It had to stop . . . didn't it?

CHAPTER THREE

True to his word, Cal knocked on her door the next morning. "Wake up, Janna. I'll start breakfast."

Janna heard him leave and opened her eyes reluctantly. As tired as she'd been the night before, she still hadn't slept well. Her emotions had been too strung up. Even when she'd managed to drift off from time to time, her dreams had been disturbing enough to bring her awake again.

She climbed out of bed and moved to the dresser mirror, wincing at the sight of her drawn features and heavy eyes. She looked awful! She grimaced at her reflection and went to the bathroom to take a shower, hoping she'd feel more alive than dead when it was over. And she did feel a little better afterward as she dressed in jeans and a yellow pullover. She crossed to the window to check on the storm before putting on makeup and combing her hair, hoping rather desperately that it had stopped and that she'd be able to leave here before it was too late to keep a rein on her feelings about Cal.

With fingers crossed, she pulled back the curtains and then held her breath in awe, delighted at what she saw. The view outside the window was that of a winter wonderland. White snow was everywhere, piled by the wind in picturesque drifts several feet deep. It came up almost to the windowsill, and if she'd opened the window, she could have reached out and scooped up a handful. Sparks glistened off icicles hanging from the house eaves as clear, bright sunlight flooded the scene, and Janna's heart beat faster in sheer joy. She felt just as she always had from the time she'd been old enough to walk. She wanted to go out in it, the sooner the better!

She whooped and giggled and turned completely around in a little dance of anticipation, unmindful of the noise she made.

"What the . . . ?" Cal came into the bedroom and stood watching her with dark eyebrows raised in astonishment. Janna didn't care that he hadn't knocked this time. Nothing could dull her spirits.

"Oh, Cal, it's gorgeous! Can we go out in it . . . is it too deep . . . do you have a sled?" She danced over to him, laughingly tugging on his arm. "Come on, Cal. Let's go outside and play!"

He was smiling back at her indulgently, taking in her sleep-tousled hair and fresh, clean face devoid of makeup. "Hold on, brown eyes. Has sleeping in this room made you regress to your childhood?"

"Yes . . . I mean, no! I mean, I'm always like this when it's like that outside!" Janna tugged coaxingly on his hand. "Oh, please, Cal. Let's go out. Don't you want to?"

Janna had no idea how charming she looked in her yellow top and jeans, brown eyes shining, and a delectable smile curving the tender fullness of her mouth. She shuffled impatiently as Cal stared hard at her, and she continued to pull on his hand. *"Please,* Cal!"

He blinked once, and then tugged on a strand of her hair. "Comb your hair, honey bear, and come to breakfast.

57

We're not going anywhere until I've had some coffee." His voice was rough, but not hostile, and Janna raced over to the dresser to pull a comb through her long tresses impatiently, then raced back to where Cal still stood watching her. "Come on, then," she teased, and laughed as he put an arm around her waist and drew her out the door with him and on to the kitchen.

Once there, he pushed her into a chair, and served up ham and eggs and delicious coffee to her groans of protest. "Eat," he ordered in a no-nonsense tone. Then he relented. "You'll need it—it's cold out there." He laughed as Janna clapped her hands in delight and proceeded to dig into the food. "We can't stay out long," he warned her. "And you'll have to put on snowshoes. The snow's too deep to get around without them." He poured her a cup of coffee and then sat down to have his own breakfast, watching her with a curious gleam in his blue eyes.

"No sledding, huh?" Janna asked and drank her coffee too fast, burning her mouth. "Ouch!" She set the cup down and fanned her mouth to cool it.

"No sledding today," Cal said firmly. "And if you don't slow down on that coffee, you won't be able to eat for a week!"

Janna grinned at him and picked up her cup again, sipping slowly this time. "Tomorrow then?"

"Tomorrow what, Janna?" Cal sounded exaggeratedly patient as if he were dealing with a four-year-old child.

"Can we sled tomorrow?" Janna was persistent.

"We'll see." Cal finished his food and stood up. "I'll get the snowshoes while you finish that."

Janna burned her mouth again once he was out of sight, but she got the coffee and the food down at last, and then hurried to the hallway to find her coat, scarf, and gloves.

Cal came to get his own while she was tucking her scarf into her collar, and she waited impatiently until he was ready.

"Let's go." Blue eyes took in her appearance and nodded in satisfaction. "You look as if you knew how to dress out here. I was afraid you wouldn't have sense enough to wrap up."

Janna stuck out her tongue at him impudently. She wasn't about to take offense and spoil their outing. He growled at her threateningly and made a move as if to chastise her, but she skipped out of his reach and headed for the door.

It was glorious outside. The temperature really was too low to stay out long, but Janna managed to enjoy what time they had. She pelted Cal with a snowball and then landed in a snowdrift in an effort to escape retaliation, losing one of her snowshoes in the process.

"Serves you right," he growled in mock severity as he pulled her out and helped her get the shoe back on. But when she would have moved away from him, he held her and dumped a handful of snow on her head, taking revenge with unholy glee.

She squealed in mock anger, and he laughed at her protests. "Didn't your mother ever teach you to pick on someone your own size?" She scolded indignantly. "You've frozen my nose!" She raised a mittened hand to rub it dry, and he laughed at the sight and pulled her close to him.

"I thought you said honey bears learned not to provoke mountain lions," he chided softly, and then their eyes caught and held, and they both sobered at once.

Janna got lost in the blue flame that came closer and closer until she felt the cold touch of his mouth on her own. His lips were soft, but demanding, then they firmed to a bruising passion that shook her to the core. And then he pushed her away from him and bent down to pick up a glove he'd dropped.

"Let's get back to the house," he said grimly. "It's too cold for you to stay out any longer."

Janna didn't argue as he took her arm and guided her back to the house. But the sunshine had gone out of her day at his quick change of mood. She thought ruefully that while she loved his touch, it was debatable whether it was worth it when he always seemed to regret his advances almost as quickly as he made them. Besides, every intimacy now would be paid for later with loneliness and heartache once she left here, and she'd had enough of both to last her for a good long while.

She took her time shedding her outer clothing, giving Cal an opportunity to finish first and leave her. He was pouring them both a hot drink when she rejoined him, and she studied his profile bleakly before speaking.

"Thanks for taking me out, Cal. It was . . . lovely."

He grunted noncommittally and thrust a cup into her hand. They drank silently, the atmosphere between them not exactly strained . . . but both of them were preoccupied with their own thoughts. Finally, Cal stood up.

"Still want to help me with my taxes?" He was calm, almost indifferent . . . very much a stranger.

"Yes." Janna copied his manner. "Let me do the dishes, and then I'll join you in the study."

He nodded his head and left her, and Janna did the chores, thinking wearily that if it were true that "unlucky in love" meant "lucky in money," then she ought to be a blooming millionaire.

60

CHAPTER FOUR

The extent of Cal's financial involvements amazed Janna. She had known he wasn't likely to be poor, but she hadn't guessed that he was actually quite wealthy. It put a further damper on her spirits. This was one more barrier between them. But her emotions were overridden by her work, and soon she was working dispassionately on the ledgers, balance sheets, and financial statements, her mind sharp and clear, her skills more than adequate to the task.

Cal sat with her for a while to answer her questions and show her his files. But at his growing restlessness, she sent him away, and he seemed relieved to go, mumbling indistinctly about things he needed to see to.

Janna worked for several hours on her own, forgetting to eat lunch or even to break for coffee as she became more and more involved in the complexity of Cal's accounts. He had several hundred acres of land in pasture for cattle along with interests in various businesses, including a feed lot and several restaurants . . . and a coal mine. Janna stiffened when she saw the name of the company that owned the mine. Cal was half-owner of the company where she was to work! So he was her employer, so to speak, she mused. She wondered what he'd do if he knew. In view of his disapproval of a woman working at a mine, would he fire her? She shrugged. Maybe it would be better if he did. When she was finally able to leave here, she didn't want to be reminded of him at every turn. It was going to be hard enough to forget him as it was.

It was late in the afternoon before Janna's aching eyes and cramped body forced her to abandon her task temporarily. But she'd accomplished most of what she'd set out to do, and she was certain Cal had nothing to fear from the tax audit. She was also convinced he needed at least a part-time bookkeeper/secretary and wondered if he did have one. The weather would have kept anyone away for the last two days.

She rose from the desk, stretched wearily, and left the study, wondering where Cal had been all day. She hadn't seen or heard from him for hours. She wandered around the house looking for him, but he wasn't to be found, so she ended up in the kitchen feeling thirsty, but not for coffee. There was a utility room and pantry off the kitchen, and Janna looked in to see if there were any soft drinks. All she found were several jugs of a pale golden liquid labeled "apple."

She brought one to the kitchen and poured a glassful. The taste was pleasingly tart and there was a slight kick to the innocent-looking beverage that puzzled her, but she was thirsty and had a couple of more glasses before she felt satisfied.

Then she moved to the room where Cal had brought her the night he'd found her. There were live coals in the grate where a fire had burned down, and Janna piled wood on to stir up a blaze before she stretched out on the sofa to relax.

Suddenly, she was strangely light-headed and giggly and her eyes fixed on the bearskin rug on the floor. She maneuvered her body carefully—somehow it wasn't behaving properly—and slipped down to lie beside the rug and stroke the hairy head. "Fuzzy Wuzzy was a worm," she chanted, then frowned, trying to concentrate. "No, I beg your pardon . . . Fuzzy Wuzzy was a bear!" That was all she could remember of the rhyme she'd repeated as a child, and she giggled and hugged the white head. "Fuzzy Wuzzy wasn't fuzzy, wuz he?' But you are, aren't you, sweetie?" She kissed the hairy cheek and then lay back flat on the hard floor, wondering why the room wasn't quite steady.

"Enjoying yourself?" Janna cocked an eye to see the slightly wavering figure of Cal Burke standing nearby watching her, an amused twist to his mouth.

"Yes," she nodded gravely and then giggled again at his slight frown. "Fuzzy and I are getting acquainted, aren't we, Fuzzy?" She tickled Fuzzy's chin, undismayed at the bear's lack of response.

Cal kneeled beside her, his eyes searching her face quizzically. "Did you by any chance raid my liquor cabinet?" he asked dryly.

Janna put both hands behind her head, crossed her ankles, and tried to whistle a tune unsuccessfully.

"Janna?" Cal reached out and turned her head to face him.

"No, I didn't raid . . . er, cabinet . . ." she said indignantly. "I only had apple juss . . . juice. It's muss . . . must . . . *much* healfier." She got the words out finally and fixed him with a reproving glare. "I don't drink, you know . . . much." She remembered that she did like a vodka collins occasionally and wine with dinner once in a while, and she wanted to be perfectly truthful.

63

"I see," he drawled. "Perhaps that explains why you're so susceptible to hard cider then."

Janna saw that she amused him for some reason she couldn't fathom, and then his words registered in her foggy brain. "Cider . . . *hard* cider?" She struggled to concentrate. "That's like alcohol, isn't it?"

"Ummm . . ." he nodded. "And I think you'd better have something to eat before Fuzzy here decides you'd make a good meal." He reached down to grasp her shoulders and help her up and at the same time she moved to sit up, so that his hand brushed the rounded swell of her breast. The cider must have affected her more than she realized because she was on fire instantly, her body an aching need, wanting only Cal's touch.

"Cal . . ." Janna's head lolled back as she breathed his name, and her brown eyes pleaded with him to touch her.

"Janna . . . damn it, Janna!" Cal's voice was strained, and he stayed motionless for a long second before his head came down to her slowly, as if drawn irresistibly to her parted lips waiting for his kiss. He brushed her mouth with his own once, twice—then with a groan, he slid down beside her to gather her into his arms. Janna let her body arch against him, wanting to feel every inch of him next to her. His hands were warm under her sweater as they stroked her skin, and her breasts tautened as his fingers moved closer, and finally covered them, causing a fire to light inside her that made her senses reel.

She thrust her own hands under his sweater to move wherever they willed, savoring the warmth of his skin against her palms. Janna was murmuring incoherently, not knowing what she was saying but aware of Cal's heightened reaction to her words of love. His hands left her breasts to grasp her hips as he moved to cover her body with his own . . . and still it wasn't enough. Janna wanted more! She wanted total surrender.

"Cal . . . please . . ." She gasped as he caught her mouth roughly, forcing her lips apart and exploring with devastating thoroughness until she thought she couldn't bear another moment without complete unity.

Cal's hand was on the zipper of her jeans when the telephone rang, a shattering sound that brought the outside world into the room where previously there had been only the two of them. Janna groaned in disappointment as Cal lifted his head, and she saw the fire die slowly from his eyes. "Don't, Cal . . . let it ring." Janna reached up to take his face in her hands and raised herself slightly to kiss him, but he moved away from her, blinking as if coming out of a daze. He released her to sit up, and Janna watched helplessly, feeling bitterly deprived as he stood up, gave her one long look and then left the room to answer the phone.

Damn, Damn, Damn! Janna sat up and held her whirling head in her hands. Why did the blasted phone have to be restored to order now of all times! As the minutes dragged by, she gradually recovered some of her equilibrium, and as her blood cooled, she was assailed once again by a sense of shame at her behavior. What was the matter with her all of a sudden? Did Cal Burke just have to kiss her to make her throw away years of propriety? He must think she was a little tramp to behave this way on two days' acquaintance! But, heaven help her, she didn't seem to be able to help herself where he was concerned.

Carefully, using the sofa as a steadying support, she stood up, bracing herself against a wave of dizziness that made the room whirl. Then she took one careful step after another in the direction of her room, thinking a shower would clear her head. Anything was worth a try rather than facing Cal in this condition.

She had almost reached her room using the wall as support when Cal came out from the kitchen. Janna winced at the cool look on his face as he watched her progress, and finally she gave up and leaned against the wall, one hand pressed to her throbbing temple.

"Do you want some help?" His tone was almost gentle, though it didn't match the look on his face at all. It was all so confusing!

"No . . . no, I think I can make it." Janna thought it best not to subject either of them to the closeness entailed in his helping her. And having said she could do it, she pushed off from the wall and tried to put her words into action. But her movement was too sudden, and the room swayed alarmingly . . . or was it her body?

Cal stepped forward quickly and caught her up in his arms. "I think you'd better forego some of that independence under the circumstances," he laughed softly, and Janna clung to his neck as the whole world rocked around her while he carried her to her room. The last thing she knew before her eyes closed in a deep sleep was that Cal had pressed his lips to her forehead and had held her against him with a curious possessiveness that was marvelously comforting. And then she knew no more.

CHAPTER FIVE

Janna opened her eyes briefly and then closed them again almost at once, a groan of misery echoing softly from her lips as a shaft of sunlight stabbed with ferocious intensity across her sensitive pupils. She lay quietly and assessed the damage. She had a splitting headache, a terrible taste in her mouth, and a pit of nausea in her stomach. Other than that, she thought philosophically, she was in great shape . . . for a corpse.

Gathering up her courage, she turned onto her back and tried again. This time she managed to keep her eyes open, but it took considerable will power to make the effort to sit up and swing her legs over the side of the bed. She stayed there momentarily, reflecting that from here on out, it would be wise to stay away from apples in any form other than straight off the tree.

Finally, she risked standing up, and when the room had settled down into its normal position, she dragged herself across to the bathroom, keeping her eyes away from the dresser mirror deliberately. Time enough to face her reflection after she'd had a shower.

She felt vaguely human after alternating hot-and-cold water in an attempt to shock her system into a semblance of normality, and after drying off, she went to the cabinet over the sink and got out a couple of aspirins. She shuddered at the taste of them, but she managed to keep them down and then studied her face in the mirror. Well, she'd looked better, she thought wryly, but at least she recognized herself.

It was only as she was starting to dress that the cold sober thought hit her like a ton of bricks. When she'd got up from the bed, she hadn't had a stitch on! That meant Cal had. . . . She sat down weakly on the edge of the bed. Was undressing her all he'd done? She thought back desperately, but the last thing she remembered was when he'd picked her up out in the hall. Somehow she couldn't imagine him taking advantage of her unconscious state. Cal Burke was a man who would demand a response to his lovemaking, and Janna had certainly been in no condition to give one. And wouldn't she know in some way? Surely there would be some physical discomfort as an aftermath of making love for the first time—but her body was such a mass of aches and pains anyway that this wasn't a reliable criteria.

Well, there was no point in worrying over it now, she thought wearily. If it had happened, it had happened—but she really didn't think it had. If his past actions were any indication to go by, he was steering clear of that kind of involvement with her. The thought brought a confusing flash of disappointment, and Janna got up and finished dressing, concentrating all of her attention on this mundane task in an effort to get away from her own thoughts.

She brushed her hair, and it crackled with electricity, so she tied it back at the nape with a scarf, then set to work with her makeup to hide the traces of dissipation her overactive conscience fancied she could detect.

She glanced at her watch to check the time, and somehow the action recalled countless other times when she'd done it to make sure she was on time for work. Work! She was supposed to have reported for work yesterday! Would she still have a job when she hadn't shown up and hadn't even called in to explain? There was only one way to find out. The phone was obviously working now, and she'd put in a call first thing.

Finally, there was no further excuse to linger in her room, so she left its sanctuary with considerable trepidation and headed for the kitchen, wondering what she was going to find to say to Cal when they met. She'd made a complete fool of herself, after all. Would he taunt her or ignore the whole thing?

She came into the kitchen and stopped short at the sight of Cal sitting at the table. He looked her up and down appraisingly before he spoke.

"Well, you look like you're going to live . . . barely." But he smiled at her, and suddenly Janna knew it was going to be all right.

"Thanks," she made a face at him. "But I won't know for sure until I've had some coffee." She sat down at the table with him and took the cup of coffee he offered her, avoiding the sardonic gleam in his eyes, and sipping the hot beverage gratefully.

"Do you want some food? You didn't have any dinner last night, you know." He was keeping a straight face, but laughter was lurking beneath the surface of his gravity. Janna set her cup down with a thump.

"I'll just have some toast," she said somewhat shortly, thinking it was all very well for him to enjoy the situation —he wasn't the one who was suffering. She was halfway out of her chair before he pushed her down with a firm hand.

"I'll get it. You take it easy until you're feeling more . . . er, like yourself."

Janna was sure now that he was enjoying the situation to the hilt—and all at her expense—and she scowled at his back for a moment before her own sense of humor took over, and she relaxed slightly. "I take it I'd better be more careful of what I take out of that pantry to drink." She tried to sound casual, but her lips were quivering on the verge of a smile.

Cal looked at her gravely, his own lips twitching suspiciously as he nodded agreement. "Especially if it's in a jug and looks deceptively innocuous," he agreed. "If I recall, the apple has been instrumental in more than one downfall."

Janna grimaced ruefully. "Well, I know one thing. If the apple in the Bible was in the form of hard cider, it's no wonder the devil got his foot in the door. That's potent stuff!"

Cal grinned openly at her and brought her toast to the table. "Feeling better?" he asked softly, as Janna eyed the toast dubiously and picked up a piece.

"Ummm, I'll survive," she said, and took a bite. It went down easier than she'd expected, and apart from a small flutter, her stomach accepted the offering with good grace. "How's the weather today? Are the roads open yet?"

Cal didn't answer immediately, and Janna looked up to surprise an enigmatic expression just disappearing from his face. He shrugged casually when he answered.

"The weather's clear, but it'll be a few days yet before you're able to travel." He settled back in his chair and stretched out his long legs, a watchful look in his eyes.

"A few days!" Janna swallowed down a gasp of dismay. "But my job! I'd better call my employer and explain my absence. I only hope . . . ." Janna looked down to hide her confusion. What did she hope? All at once the job she'd looked forward to didn't appeal to her nearly as much as staying here with Cal. But that was utterly foolish! He didn't want her here!

"What's the matter, Janna?" Cal's voice was cool. "Are you afraid if you stay here much longer, you won't leave in the same condition as when you came?"

There was a frostiness in his blue eyes that chilled her, and she flinched at his words. So he couldn't resist bringing up her shameful behavior of the day before. It was obvious what he thought of her. But she'd asked for his opinion by her actions, hadn't she?

"I'm merely anxious to get out from under your feet and to leave you in peace and get on with my own life," she said hesitantly. "I know I'm not an easy guest to have." She stopped talking, and with as much dignity as she could muster, she got to her feet. "If you'll excuse me, I'll make that call."

"Call who you like!" Cal pushed his chair back almost violently, stood, then walked to the door. He stopped there and glared at her. "Just remember, if things don't turn out as you expect, I'm available for other kinds of help besides rescuing snow bunnies!"

He left the room, and Janna took a deep breath, wondering what on earth he'd meant by that remark. He was as hard to understand as . . . as any other man!

Feeling unaccountably cross and out of sorts, she picked up the phone and dialed her employer. Seconds later, she was listening with disbelief to her erstwhile employer politely but firmly dispense with her services. Desperately, she tried to explain. "But I couldn't help being delayed, Mr. Sanderson," she protested. "Please, won't you give me a chance?"

But the man was adamant. He'd already replaced her—with a male accountant, of course—and it was too late to change now. He was barely polite, and it was evident that he was delighted with the turn of events. He rang off with an alacrity that was just short of rudeness, and Janna looked at the dead phone in her hand and uttered a very unladylike expletive.

Oh, damn, damn, damn, she thought furiously. What was she going to do now? Her funds would barely stretch to last another two weeks, and she'd counted on that job to support her literally as well as emotionally. Returning home didn't appeal at all, even though her previous heartache over Frank seemed to have miraculously disappeared since she'd met Cal. In fact, it looked as though she might very well have taken a flying leap out of the frying pan and into the fire in the love department. But a fat lot of good that did her. Cal thought she was a cross between a teenage menace and a high-class . . . Janna stifled the thought before it broke completely through. What was the use of condemning herself when she had Cal to do it for her?

She was back to banging dishes around in the sink when she had the sensation of being watched and swung around to find Cal leaning against the door frame, a sardonic smile on his lips. "My, my, what's got you in a temper again?" he drawled.

Janna had the irrational thought for a moment that he looked pleased about something, but the suspicion was swallowed up in her anger.

"I've lost my job because of this damned storm, that's what! But you'll be happy to know that my replacement is a man, and therefore entirely suitable for the position.

72

I only hope he breaks a leg!" She swung back to the sink, feeling foolish at her childish remark, but still in a temper and unwilling to let go of it.

Cal came to stand beside her and took up a drying towel, whistling softly and infuriatingly and ignoring the glares she threw in his direction. It was inevitable the way she was handling the dishes that she break something eventually, but when she did, it affected her out of all proportion to its importance. It was the proverbial last straw, in fact, and she burst into tears and flung her sponge into the dish water, preparing to storm out the door in a fury of frustration and disappointment.

Cal caught her around the waist with ease, effectively stopping her flight. "Take it easy, sweetheart." He pulled her into his arms and rocked her consolingly, causing her to cry all the harder because of his sympathy. "Get it out then," he murmured in her ear, his strong hands trailing fire over her back and shoulders. "Cry it out, baby."

Janna positively wailed at that. Here she was running away from a broken engagement only to lose her job and her heart in less than a week and trying her best to lose her virginity in the process. It was just too much, and she sobbed in self-pity until there wasn't a tear left in her.

Once again the handkerchief came out and Cal was drying her eyes. "This is getting to be a habit, hmmm?" He shook her gently as the tears threatened again. "Come on, Janna, it's not that bad. You've got the qualifications to get another job."

Janna sniffed, but she didn't resist when he drew her back into his arms. "How do you know what my qualifications are," she asked sulkily. "You think I'm just good for cooking and cleaning!" She sniffed again self-pityingly, and Cal looked at her indulgently, one eyebrow raised.

73

"Did I say that?" he drawled. And at her indignant nod he added, "Well, if I did, I've changed my mind after seeing what you did with my tax records. You've about got them licked into shape, haven't you?"

Janna shot him a suspicious look through her tears, tilting her head back to see his expression, but he pressed her face back into his shoulder.

"As a matter of fact," he continued teasingly, "if you ask me nicely, I might consider taking you on full time. I need an accountant. Things are getting out of hand."

Janna drew back abruptly, appalled at the idea of spending her days keeping his books straight for the privilege of mooning over him silently. It would never work. He'd end up showing her the door once he got tired of having a lovesick female around his house all day. She couldn't bear that.

"Oh, no!" Her words came out with a sharp intensity, and she bit her lip in consternation. "I mean . . . I couldn't . . . you don't . . . you don't need someone full time anyway—not yet." Seconds later, Janna was astounded at his angry reaction to her refusal to consider his idea.

"So all your fine words about gratitude were just that— words!" He thrust her away from him, his face a hard mask of anger and contempt.

Janna floundered in confusion. "Gratitude?" She faltered. "What's gratitude got to do with it?"

"Oh, hell, not a thing," he said sarcastically. "Just because I saved your life doesn't mean you owe me a thing. Forget all about it, by all means!"

He started past her, and Janna caught his arm, her expression plainly showing her confusion and chagrin. "But of course I'm grateful, Cal," she stammered. "I just didn't think you really wanted . . . or needed . . . anything from me."

He seemed a little mollified by her words, but he still eyed her calculatingly. "Yes, well, you were wrong. I need an accountant, and I thought you'd be willing to stay on here and help me out, but I guess it's asking too much." He made as if to brush by her again, but Janna held on to his arm, her eyes wide and earnest as she looked pleadingly at him.

"Oh, Cal, of course I'll do it if you want me to. I'm sorry. I thought you were just offering me the job out of . . ." She stopped, unwilling to put into words an emotion she wanted no part of where Cal Burke was concerned.

"Out of what?" He prompted her roughly.

"To be nice," she prevaricated. "Because I lost my job."

He took hold of her again and forced her chin up so that she had to look at him. "When you get to know me better, Janna, you'll find I'm not that nice. In fact, I can be downright ruthless in getting what I want. Remember that."

Janna blinked as he bent his head and brushed her lips with his own before letting her go. "You start as of today . . . as soon as you finish those dishes." He laughed lightly at her mutinous glance at the sink and moved to the door. "Come to the study when you're finished here. Oh, and bring a pot of coffee. There's a lot more hidden away in there than just tax work, and you're going to earn every penny I pay you!"

Janna stared at his retreating back, feeling distinctly manipulated, but unable to put her finger on any justification for her intuitive suspicion. Why should Cal manipulate her to stay here with him? He could have taken her and hadn't, so it was fairly obvious that she didn't attract him enough to make that the reason. She was probably just being fanciful. It was just as likely that he did need an accountant and that he was impressed with her work and had decided to take advantage of the fact that she was already here and available to do it. And she supposed she owed him that, in all fairness. But it wasn't going to be easy. No, it wasn't going to be easy at all.

CHAPTER SIX

Two days later, as Janna was adding a column of figures at top speed, she reflected somewhat wearily that Cal had meant it when he'd said she would earn her pay. His own limitless energy was carrying her along in its path until she was hard put to keep up—and she had never been a shirker, nor was she afraid of hard work.

Cal was all business with her now. He didn't joke, he didn't touch her, and he didn't make small talk. He just kept shoveling work at her as if they were two automatons. The only saving grace was that he also had an uncanny ability to sense when she was at the end of her rope temporarily, at which time he would suggest a break for coffee or a meal.

They took turns cooking, and their meals were eaten quickly as if there were a deadline to meet. It was still impossible to leave the house except for very brief excursions in pursuit of exercise, and Janna's nerves were tightening with the cabin fever Cal had mentioned. She knew it was aggravated by having to work side by side with him, and having to hide her reactions when his every movement set her pulses racing.

Now she finished adding figures and stood to stretch her tired muscles and rub her aching neck. She hoped she'd feel better when the snow melted and she was able to get out and away from him for a few hours a day—and especially when she was able to find somewhere else to sleep! Having him two doors down from her own room gave her instant insomnia!

Cal looked up from where he sat on the sofa in front of the fire studying a file. "Time for coffee?" he asked and rose and stretched his own muscles and Janna's throat tightened.

Janna cleared the sudden huskiness from her throat. "Yes. I'll get it."

"Fine," he said absently, and settled back down to his file. Janna left the room feeling decidedly cross. She could barely get Cal to acknowledge her presence, much less give her the kind of attention she wanted from him. Even the realization that in the long run, she would have reason to be grateful for his indifference did little to assuage her longing for a closer relationship.

In her heart Janna didn't really want an affair with Cal. She knew it would set the seal on the love she felt hovering just on the edge of her consciousness, and which her common sense told her would be disastrous to give in to. So, of course, it was better to continue this barren employer/employee relationship. It was just that her common sense could go flying away on the wings of desire when she was forced to spend hour after hour close to this man whose very voice could send shivers of yearning right through her.

When she came back with a tray of coffee, Cal mumbled his thanks, and Janna took her own cup to a chair a safe distance away from him. She sipped the coffee slowly and studied Cal covertly from under her lashes.

He never talked about himself, and she had yet to find

out why his niece had a bedroom in his house. What she really wanted to know was how a man with so much to offer had escaped marriage. She supposed he could have been married before and was now divorced, but she hadn't come across anything in his business papers that would indicate such was the case. The only thing she knew for certain was that she herself had no chance of becoming Mrs. Cal Burke—not that she wanted to, she told herself somewhat untruthfully. But since he wasn't even interested enough in her to take advantage of having her at his mercy in his own home, there was little likelihood that he had anything more permanent in mind. All the same, she thought rather wistfully, he would probably make a good husband for someone sometime.

"How's it coming, Janna?" Cal set the file aside and looked at her.

Janna started guiltily at his question. Thank goodness, she'd taken her eyes off him only seconds before, or he would have surprised her watching him and perhaps drawn the wrong conclusions—or the right ones, depending on the point of view, she thought ruefully.

"I'll be through with *this* project this afternoon," she answered him, half-hoping there wouldn't be another to take its place. Perhaps if there weren't, he would consider her obligation to him discharged and let her go. But Cal killed that hope with his next words.

"Good. I've got something else I want to start you on tomorrow."

Janna closed her eyes wearily. Just how many projects was he going to have, she thought a little desperately, only to have him answer that question too.

"The weather report says a thaw should set in in a couple of days. Then we can start getting you settled in."

Janna sat up abruptly. "Settled in?" She had thought she was about as settled as she was ever going to be, at least when dealing with Cal Burke.

"Yes. I've got a little cottage about a mile down the road. It needs some fixing up, but you can do that in your spare time—you know, curtains, rugs, and the like. You can use my accounts at stores in Cheyenne to buy whatever you need." Cal picked up the file he'd put aside and began to leaf through it as if the subject were closed, but Janna thought there was a tenseness about him that belied his casualness. For her part, she was simply flabbergasted. While it would be nice to get out of this house and away from him, she hadn't planned on spending her whole life here!

"Er, Cal." Janna took a deep breath as he looked up at her blandly. Drat him, he knew she wouldn't let his bombshell pass without comment, so why was he affecting this unconcerned attitude? "Let me get this straight," she said almost grimly. "Are you saying I'm to live in this cottage and continue to work for you . . . full time!?"

Cal frowned in annoyance. "Of course. You accepted the job, didn't you? And it's too far for you to live in town. The cottage is there, and it's empty. You might as well make use of it." He eyed her cynically. "It's a little far from the bright lights and there won't be much social life—but it has its compensations. No traffic jams, no hectic rushing around—and the peace and quiet of the Wyoming countryside, not to mention its beauty, has never bored me. Is that what's bothering you? Afraid you'll be bored?" He said the last rather accusingly, and Janna swallowed down a retort that she wasn't likely to be bored with him around; in fact, quite the opposite.

She'd had almost a surfeit of the kind of excitement he created.

"No . . . no, it isn't that!" She sounded overly emphatic, but it was too late to call the words back.

"Well, what is it then?" Cal's impatience was marked, but Janna had a sudden picture of herself sitting here twenty years from now, still fascinated by him, still suffering from his indifference . . . in short, a dried-up old maid suffering from unrequited love—unless one got over such things as one got older . . . or unless he got married.

She jumped up in dismay and turned her back to him, facing the crackling fire in a panic. "It's just that I thought . . . I didn't think . . ." Oh, how did she say it without really saying it!

Cal got up and came to stand beside her, taking her chin in his hand to force her head up so he could see her expression. His own expression was ruthless. "What is it you thought . . . or didn't think, Janna?" His posture and his voice expressed determination, and Janna looked at him as if at a stranger. And of course that's what he was . . . and a ruthless one at that.

"I didn't think you really meant that I was to continue working for you once the roads are clear and I can leave here." She tried to sound businesslike, but a note of pleading crept through. It left him unmoved.

"Well, you were wrong." The frost in his eyes was chilling. "You accepted this job, and I don't recall that any time limit was specified. Unless you've decided that two days' work satisfies your debt to me." His tone was sarcastic and it made Janna recoil. It was obvious he was going to keep her tied to him, regardless of her own wishes, by continually bludgeoning her with how much she owed him. And Janna knew that he would automatically win any argument between them with such tactics—her own conscience would be his ally. It puzzled her even while it made her rage in futile indignation. She could have sworn Cal wasn't the type to demand gratitude for what he'd done, and his behavior seemed so uncharacteristic, but then she didn't know him well enough to be that sure of his character.

"Well, Janna?" Cal was prompting her to a response, a crisp note of purposefulness in his voice that sealed her defeat. "What's it to be?" he persisted. "Are you going to run out on me or honor your commitments?"

Janna shrugged helplessly. "I'll stay as long as you need me, Cal." And to herself, she added silently, "or as long as I can stand it—whichever comes first."

"Good. I'll hold you to that." There was a self-satisfied note in his voice that brought Janna's head up in time to see what looked suspiciously like a gleam of triumph in Cal's blue eyes, but it was gone so quickly that she couldn't be sure she hadn't imagined it. And then he moved away from her toward the door. "I have some calls to make. If you need me, I'll be in the kitchen."

Janna watched him go, her temper rising now that she'd committed herself to a course of action that she was certain was absolutely wrong for her. Damn Cal! Was he the type who'd run roughshod over anyone to suit himself—or was he being genuinely kind in insisting she take this job? Maybe he thought she couldn't get another job—that she wasn't good enough! But that thought made her even angrier. Well, she'd stick it out as long as she could, but if her feelings ever got to the point where she felt she couldn't bear being around him any longer, she'd leave . . . and to the devil with gratitude!

With the added impetus of her anger spurring her on,

she went back to the job at hand and tackled it with ferocious concentration, finding solace in performing the work she was trained for and in performing it well. At least Cal Burke would have no cause for complaint concerning her skills—it was as a woman that he might just find he had his hands full!

CHAPTER SEVEN

The next morning was April 1, and as Janna pulled back her bedroom curtains in her daily ritual to check on the weather, she felt her heart leap in gratitude. April Fools' Day was here with a vengeance and was forcing winter to give way to spring. The sun was back on the job, and already had the icicles melting with encouraging plops. The thought that it wouldn't be long before she could move out of Cal's home was like a breath of fresh air. She'd had about all she could stand of lying awake nights knowing he was just down the hall within easy reach.

The man occupying her thoughts tapped on her door, and Janna acknowledged his call with a secret smile of relief. Soon she'd be spared the devastating intimacy of that knock.

"Coming!" She crossed the room and swung open the door with a flourish, only to stop short when she found Cal waiting for her. "Oh! Good morning!" She gave him a dazzling smile. She could afford to let down her guard a little now that relief from his overwhelming presence was within sight.

"Good morning, Janna," he drawled lazily, taking in her good mood in a glance. "You're certainly sparkling today—couldn't be the change in the weather, could it?"

She shot him a mischievous look, daring even to tease in her excess of good spirits. "Of course, it could," she said flippantly. "Cabin fever had me almost begging for a ray of sunshine and my prayers have been answered!"

She swung off down the hall, flashing him a grin over her shoulder. "And I'll bet you're just as glad as I am for the thaw. Now you can have your house to yourself again without me underfoot. You can't pretend that won't be a relief!"

Cal followed her into the kitchen, one eyebrow cocked quizzically. "Now I wonder why you'd feel that way. Have I ever said I minded having you here? I thought I'd gone out of my way to be the perfect host." There was a dry self-mockery behind his words that would have alerted Janna to a deeper meaning had she been less carried away by her own enthusiasm. But in her present mood the subtle nuance passed her by.

"Oh, you have been the perfect host," she said airily. "But everyone knows crusty old bachelors don't like their privacy invaded, especially by damsels in distress—and most especially by damsels in distress who turn out to have nasty tempers and a penchant for hard cider!" She laughed gaily to cover her sudden confusion at this mention of the day she'd behaved like a wanton under the influence of alcohol—not that she'd needed alcohol to release her inhibitions. Cal Burke's touch was enough of a stimulant in itself!

"Is that how you see me?" he asked casually. "As a crusty old bachelor?" He fixed her in a blue gleam that threatened to show her he was nothing of the sort, but Janna shook her head, reflecting quite truthfully that he was the opposite of that characterization if anything.

"Well, perhaps not," she teased. "You're not old, for

85

one thing. And you're only crusty sixteen hours out of the day that I know of—but you are a bachelor!"

Cal chuckled. "Sixteen hours a day, hmmm? Maybe one of these days I'll show you how nice I can be during the other eight. You might be surprised." His voice was lazily seductive, and for the first time in days, he allowed his eyes to travel over her with heart-stopping thoroughness.

At his words and his look, Janna almost swallowed a bite of toast whole, and she dissolved into a fit of choking that she hoped covered her confusion.

Cal reached over and pounded her back none too gently until she cringed away from him, whereupon he laughed at her softly, a wicked light in his eyes. "You should remember not to bite off more than you can chew, Janna. In more ways than one," he murmured exasperatingly.

Janna pretended to take a sip of coffee to clear her throat, but in reality she was hoping to hide the fact that her pulses were racing madly with joy at his return to the intimate teasing she'd missed so much. But she couldn't let him know that. It probably meant nothing to him.

"Do you have any idea when we can reach my car . . . and when I can move out?" Her defensive retreat was blatantly obvious and she could see it amused him.

"Oh, I'd say it'll be a couple of days yet. Think you can stand it?" He kept his tone bland, but Janna was aware of the intensity with which he watched her.

"Sure," she shrugged. "If I've stood it this long . . ." She stopped, horrified at her unthinking admission. But it was preferable for him to think her words were the result of rudeness rather than guess at her real meaning.

But Cal seemed unperturbed and his smile was suddenly satisfied and mysterious. Janna had the sinking feeling that he knew just exactly what she'd meant, and his reply seemed to confirm her fears.

"Cheer up, honey bear," he said caressingly. "You'll be out of the lion's den in no time. But if you really knew anything about creatures of the wild, you might not be so eager to go. Sometimes it's safer to be actually in a hunter's lair than out in the open where he has a clear field."

Having delivered himself of that startling observation, he stood up and tugged at a strand of her hair as he passed her to go to the porch. "I'm going out to check on storm damage. There's a file on my desk for you to work on. See you."

He went out whistling cheerfully, leaving Janna bewildered, but with an underlying excitement that wouldn't be denied. She didn't dare examine the reasons for that excitement too closely, but it was with a lightened heart and a song on her lips that she faced the tasks of the day, feeling life might just be worthwhile after all. No doubt it was the weather, she told herself with blithe unconcern for truthfulness. Sunshine made everyone's day seem brighter.

CHAPTER EIGHT

Janna surveyed her new home with a dawning delight. True, it needed cleaning and some decorative touches here and there, but she could already see the possibilities in her own mind. It was just her size—one small sitting room, a bedroom, bathroom, and kitchen. The furnishings were Early American, and while she normally preferred something more modern, in this house the pieces fit the atmosphere and she knew she wouldn't change them.

"Do you like it?" Cal wandered to a charming maple rocking chair and sat down.

"Yes." Janna answered him simply with the one word, but there was a wealth of meaning in her tone and in the pleased sparkle of her eyes.

Cal leaned back and surveyed her as she stooped to run her fingers appreciatively over the polished hardwood floor. "You won't be lonely here?" he queried musingly, a brooding look darkening the blue of his eyes momentarily.

"Oh, I don't think so," she replied happily. A sudden thought struck her. "Cal, do you realize this will be my very first place that's all my own? I've always lived with my parents before. And I couldn't have found a more charming place to begin." She went to the flowered sofa and bounced a couple of times before settling back to survey her future domain with pleased satisfaction.

"Ummm . . ." Cal watched her with an indulgent smile. "Just a little homebody, were you?" he asked casually.

"Well, no. I wanted to move out," she answered him seriously. "But my parents were so delighted to have me with them that I couldn't find the heart to leave them . . . not even for Frank . . ." She stopped, wishing she hadn't inadvertently mentioned her former fiancé. Hoping Cal would let it pass, she rushed on. "I went to college in my hometown, you see, so there wasn't even a chance to go away then."

"Who's Frank?" Cal asked the question softly, but there was a dangerous note in his voice that made Janna uneasy.

"Er, a friend," she said reluctantly.

"Just a friend, Janna?" Cal was persistent and Janna jumped up to move around the room, feeling curiously nervous.

"Janna?" The note of danger was stronger now, and Janna stopped her pacing to eye him warily.

"Well, actually, he was my fiancé," she said offhandedly, but her voice cracked and it didn't come off as she'd intended.

"And what happened to this fiancé?" Cal was tensely alert now, and the blue of his eyes glinted sharply.

"He decided my best friend suited him better," Janna confessed wryly, still surprised that since meeting Cal, the matter of Frank and Mellie's defection left her almost unmoved.

"When was this?" Cal's questions were taking on the aspect of an inquisition, and Janna frowned.

"Just before I came out here," she answered him shortly. "And if you don't mind, I'd rather not . . ."

89

"Ahhh," Cal relaxed his body, but his eyes were still alert and still dangerous. "So that's why you finally left Mom and Dad and came out here on your own?"

"Yes!" Janna's temper was on the rise now, and she felt more able to give rein to it now that she was out of Cal's immediate domain. "And I don't see why you're so interested. I'd like to drop the subject if you don't mind?"

Cal got up from his chair and came to stand close to her. "Yes, we will forget it, Janna . . . both of us." There was a grim note in his voice that puzzled and annoyed her. Why should he care about her past love life? "Well, all right then," she said irritably and started to move past him to look into the bedroom. She wanted to see if there were linens already there, or if she'd have to borrow some from Cal until she could buy some of her own.

"Janna?" There was a warning note in Cal's voice now and she stopped to look at him, wondering what the matter was this time. "Is there any chance this Frank might change his mind about this friend of yours?"

"No!" Her answer was firm and unequivocal.

"How can you be sure?" He took her shoulders into his hands and gave her an impatient shake.

"Because he and Mellie were married three weeks ago," she retorted and tried to pull away. Really, he was like a bull dog when he got onto a subject.

Cal amazed her then by bursting into a gleeful laugh. She gave him a cold glare. "Well, I'm glad you think it's funny," she said haughtily.

Cal drew her resisting body to him and wrapped his arms around her, giving her a tight squeeze before drawing back slightly. "I'm just relieved that I'm not going to lose the best accountant I ever had," he mocked her. He chuckled again, a wicked gleam lighting his eyes as he saw

90

the mutiny reflected plainly on her face. "Why did you think I was so interested, honey bear?" He pulled her closer to him again, and Janna brought up her hands to his chest to push him away. But he wasn't having any of her resistance.

"Answer me, Janna," he murmured as he tilted her chin up to bring her mouth close to his own.

"I . . . I don't know," Janna said breathlessly. She wished desperately that Cal wouldn't play these games with her. Did he just like to make sure he could still exercise his power over her?

"Well, think about it, hmmm? Maybe when you're all tucked up in your safe little bed in your safe little house tonight."

He kissed her then, and Janna wanted to resist, but the moment his mouth touched hers, she was lost in a dream world of desire. She found her arms moving of their own volition to circle his neck while her lips parted yearningly under the increasing pressure of his. She felt as if she'd been starving, and he was her sustenance. When he molded her against his body with hard, experienced hands, she yielded willingly, trembling at the touch of his hard thighs against her own. He kissed her roughly, demandingly, until she was gasping for breath, and then he dragged his mouth away to nuzzle her neck, bending her backwards to reach her throat and wringing a moan from the very depths of her being with the touch of his hands on her breasts.

"Janna . . . Janna," he murmured hoarsely. "God, you don't know how hard it's been to keep from doing this to you—but I had to wait . . ."

Janna moved to kiss the warm brown column of his throat, and lowered her arms to unbutton his shirt with trembling fingers. She wanted to touch his skin—to torture him a little perhaps as he had tortured her, and was still torturing her. "Why did you have to wait, Cal," she said shudderingly, accusingly, as she slipped her hands into the opening of his shirt to run her palms caressingly over the smooth skin of his chest and through the dark hair that invited her touch. "You knew I wanted you— you still know it."

"For the simple reason that I wanted you to be able to answer truthfully that your stay in my house was innocent in every way," Cal forced her head up to look into her eyes, his own darkening even further when he saw the drugged quiescence reflected there. "But you're not likely to be asked about your stay in this house, and that sets me free to pursue you in the way I've wanted to since the moment I rescued you." He kissed her eyes and then teased her lips with his own. "You're going to be in need of rescue from me from now on, Janna Wilding," he murmured huskily against her mouth. "Do you want to be rescued?" His tongue traced her lips, and all Janna was capable of was a very weak shake of her head. "So be it then," he said very softly, and Janna felt trapped in the shimmery glisten of blue eyes that told her plainly that she was his—and that he intended to claim his property.

His lovemaking took on a subtle possessiveness and a subdued violence then. And Janna was shaken by the new power he exerted that had her responding in ways she'd never dreamed existed until she was leaning against him in a weakened submission that drew a pleased and triumphant laugh that was almost a growl from the depths of his chest. He seemed in no hurry to claim his prize— seemingly content that it was there to be had. But even his formidable control was nearing its end, and Janna felt a triumph of her own as his ragged breathing quickened and his eyes glazed with desire.

"Janna, sweet—let me show you . . ."

Janna was not to know the satisfaction of what Cal wanted to show her, however. The toot of a horn in the drive outside came as an unwelcome interruption that shattered the promise of heaven to come. Cal stiffened and raised his head in angry inquiry. The toot came again, and he reluctantly pushed her slightly away from him. But his hands and his eyes held her a moment longer before he let her go. "We don't seem to be fated for intimate moments together, do we, sweetheart?" he muttered grimly as he raised a hand to rub the back of his neck frustratedly. He smiled at her possessively, and then ruefully. "Remember where we were while I see who this is. I'll get rid of them."

Janna nodded dumbly, feeling as limp as a rag doll from the effects of his lovemaking—and fully as frustrated as Cal had seemed at the interruption of that lovemaking. But she had enough presence of mind to grab up her purse and head for the bathroom in case whoever it was insisted on coming into the house. One look at her in her present state and the unwelcome visitor would have little doubt of what had been taking place.

Cal had barely reached the door when there was the sound of quick steps coming up onto the porch, then he opened the door, and Janna heard a female voice crying his name. "Cal, darling!" The endearment stopped Janna in her tracks just inside the bedroom door. It might mean nothing, but she couldn't resist eavesdropping for a moment.

"Lisa!" Cal sounded slightly taken aback. And more importantly, he didn't sound displeased at all at the identity of the visitor. Janna's lips tightened as a long silence followed his greeting. If they weren't kissing, then what were they doing? She slipped through the bedroom and on into the bathroom, locking the door behind her. She stood staring with unseeing eyes at the mirror above the sink, a sick feeling taking possession of her. What had she expected? she asked herself scornfully. That Cal was a monk —with his looks and assets? Or that the fact that he was willing to make love to his employee meant any more than that he was a normal man with normal instincts? How naive could she get? And she was past the age where it was excusable.

Janna could hear muffled voices in the living room, and she fumbled in her purse for a comb and lipstick. Whoever this Lisa was, she apparently intended to prolong her visit, and Janna had no intention of skulking in the bathroom until she did leave—nor did she intend to indicate by her appearance or by her actions that she was anything other than Cal Burke's employee.

She looked disgustedly at her tangled hair and swollen lips, all her pleasure in Cal's embraces dissipated by the knowledge that they'd meant nothing more to him than a pleasing pastime. And beneath the disgust, a familiar pain was growing—only this time she knew with certainty that the pain wouldn't be pushed out of mind through the simple expedient of finding another attractive male to fall in love with. She'd had enough love—or the lack of it—to last her a lifetime.

Seconds later she critically surveyed the effects of the repairs to her appearance and decided she'd pass . . . barely. Then she deliberately schooled her features into cool formality and left the room to join Cal and Lisa. Her surface composure almost deserted her when she stepped into the living room to find a small, dark . . . and incredibly beautiful Lisa clinging to Cal's arm and pouting prettily up into his face.

"Oh, Cal darling, why . . . ?" she was saying and then stopped when Janna came into the room. Janna came forward to be introduced, and forced a smile glued to her mouth. Yet it took less effort to be hypocritically polite than she'd expected.

The woman smiled back, but it was obvious from the cold look in her eyes that she didn't find the meeting a pleasant one. "Why, hello there," she said with false friendliness that almost made Janna wince visibly. "You must be Janna Wilding, Cal's new employee. He's been telling me about you."

Janna wondered sourly if he'd also taken the trouble to tell her that he'd been making wild love to his employee only moments before. Somehow, she didn't think that he had!

Lisa let go of Cal's arm reluctantly and stepped forward to shake hands. Janna responded by taking her hand in a firm grip and shaking it briefly, nauseated by the limp response Lisa gave. "Yes, I am," she said dryly with a brief, impersonal glance at Cal. He was watching her with cool calculation, a strange glint buried deep within the blue of his eyes.

"I'm Lisa Bower," the woman went on, with a naughty look at Cal as she moved back to take possession of his arm again. "Cal and I are old, old friends." Her intonation on the word "friends" was calculated to imply that they were much more to one another than that. "Aren't we, darling?" Lisa gave a trilling laugh and looked at Cal with intimate possessiveness.

Janna didn't move a muscle as Cal smiled down at Lisa indulgently and nodded. My, but he's cool, Janna thought with an almost calm detachment. But then I'm only his employee—he doesn't have to worry about *my* reaction.

"It's nice to meet you, Miss Bower," Janna replied quietly. She thought she sounded the epitomy of a cool, efficient employee who knew her place. Ignoring Cal's lifted eyebrow, she concentrated on Lisa Bower.

"I hope you don't mind if I hurry Cal along, Janna," Lisa said condescendingly. "But it's been days since we've had a chance to be together, and if we could get you settled in, he'll be able to come home with me for dinner."

Cal frowned, but Janna cut in before he could speak. "Of course I don't mind, Miss Bower. I'll just get my things from the Jeep and then you and Mr. Burke can leave immediately." To herself, she added silently, and the sooner the better! She shot Cal a cold look, and his blue eyes glared back at her.

"Excuse me, won't you?" Janna walked to the door and left the house with admirable eqanimity, even managing to quell the impulse to slam the door behind her. Which was just as well, because Cal was right on her heels and Lisa was on his.

The Jeep was parked so close to the house that Janna hoped Cal wouldn't have an opportunity to say anything to her for fear of Lisa overhearing. But she reckoned without his ability to get his own way.

"Go back in the house and wait, Lisa. It's chilly out here. We'll join you in a moment." He smiled to take the sting out of his words, but Lisa was clearly displeased, although she obeyed him without comment. Then Cal turned his attention to Janna.

"Proud of yourself?" He gritted the words out with controlled violence, his face a study in grimness as he bent beside her to fetch her bags from the Jeep.

"You bet I am!" She hissed the words at him. "And from now on, I'm going to continue to be. I've had a regrettable lapse in that quality lately, but that's going to change, starting right now!" She drew back from the Jeep with a bag in her hand, but he barred her way, his eyes narrowed and hard.

"Do you always jump to conclusions on so little evidence?" He was angry, but Janna didn't care.

"Depends on what you call a *little* evidence," she said coldly. "In this case, I'd say men have been hanged on less. Now get out of my way! We're keeping Miss Bower waiting." She faced him squarely, brown eyes flashing fire, and he straightened slowly, an enigmatic glint in his eye.

"By all means, Miss Wilding," he drawled cooly, and he stepped back to let her pass him.

Once back in the house, Janna smiled briefly and insincerely at Lisa Bower who was eyeing her suspiciously and who didn't bother to return the smile. But her attitude changed dramatically once Cal had brought in the rest of Janna's bags and some kitchen supplies to get her by until she could shop. Lisa even relaxed her vigilance sufficiently to leave first in order to start dinner for her "darling Cal."

Janna grimaced behind their backs as Cal escorted Lisa to her car, and then she shut the door on them and relaxed her stiff bravery into defeated anguish for a moment before dragging herself forward to put her things away. She was determinedly disciplining her emotions to deal with the reality of the mundane chores to be accomplished, when she heard the front door open behind her. She swung around in startled surprise to find Cal entering the house again.

"What do you want?" she snapped at him, bristling instantly into defiance.

"I just wanted to make sure you understand I'm expecting you to be at work tomorrow morning," he drawled lazily, and Janna colored furiously at the callousness he was displaying.

"And how am I supposed to get there?" she said sarcastically. "My car is still stuck out on the highway as far as I know."

He smiled slowly and shook his head. "No, it isn't. It's being fixed, and one of my men will have it here within the hour." He quirked an eyebrow as her mouth fell open. "Tut, tut, Miss Wilding. I'm glad it's too cold for the flies yet, or you might catch one in that lovely mouth."

Janna closed her mouth with a snap. "Well, you might have told me about the car before now," she said angrily.

"You didn't ask," he shrugged nonchalantly, and turned to the door. "Be there at eight sharp, Janna . . . or I'll come and get you. And that's a promise!" He looked as if he meant what he said, and Janna felt impotently infuriated at his arrogant assumption that he could still order her around.

"Janna?" Cal's tone brooked no defiance, and Janna turned sharply away from him to hide the fact that she was on the verge of tears.

"All right!" She almost shouted it at him. "Now will you please leave?"

There was silence behind her for a brief space before she heard the door open and Cal's soft farewell, "Good night, little honey bear," preceded its closing.

And Janna was left with only her thoughts to keep her company. And they proved less than comforting all through the long night.

CHAPTER NINE

The first thing that caught Janna's eyes on Cal's desk the next morning was an employment contract. And her own name took pride of place as the employee! She frowned and picked it up, finding to her dismay that the contract committed her to Cal Burke for the period of one year! The salary was more than generous, and she was to have the cottage rent free—but the only thing that stuck in her mind was that he was taking this route to insure that she stayed on. Why? Was it so hard to get someone to live in this isolated area? Or was it that Janna had other things to offer besides accounting skills and had made it plain that she wasn't reluctant to do so?

Janna's cheeks flamed at the thought. Was Cal, after all, just one of those employers who made a nuisance of themselves with their female employees—who wanted to have his cake and eat it too? And if Lisa Bower hadn't put in an appearance, Janna would have fallen for it hook, line, and sinker. Cal wouldn't even have had to exert his considerable powers of persuasion to get the contract signed if Lisa hadn't interrupted them yesterday. By this morning Janna would have been committed heart and soul to the philandering beast!

She threw the contract down on the desk and picked up

the file she'd been working on earlier in the week, fully intending to have the matter of her employment out with Cal as soon as he put in an appearance. This would be her last day on the job and that was final! Meanwhile, she'd clear up the few odds and ends her conscience dictated that she get out of the way before leaving for good.

Keeping one ear tuned for Cal's step, Janna worked steadily at the task, expecting at any moment to have him come into the room and mentally preparing herself for the ordeal of an ensuing argument. But as ten o'clock came and went, and he hadn't appeared, she stopped for coffee, wondering rather desperately where he could be. It was becoming quite exhausting keeping herself geared up for the showdown, only to have it delayed.

She left the study and listened for any sound of him, but the house was quiet. Gathering her courage, she walked down the corridor to his room, thinking he might still be asleep. There was no telling how late he'd been with Lisa the night before—and he might be exhausted from the reunion, she thought sourly, and might have overslept.

She knocked, and upon receiving no reply, she hesitantly opened the door. It was somewhat of an anticlimax to find the room empty, although the bed had been slept in, she noted with unwilling relief. So where was he, she fumed impotently. At that moment, she heard the telephone ring, and she backed out of Cal's room to answer it, thinking it was probably Lisa Bower checking on her darling Cal. She picked up the receiver with reluctance.

"Janna?" It was Cal, and his voice was just as disturbing over the telephone as she remembered it in person. Janna paused a moment to gather her courage. Perhaps it was better to tell him now rather than waiting until she was actually with him to do it. Even knowing what she did,

Janna felt unsure of her ability to say good-bye with any degree of conviction.

"Janna, are you there?" The rough tones were impatient —but was there an underlying note of concern as well?

Janna cleared her throat. "Yes. Where are you, Cal?" She fully expected him to say he was with Lisa Bower, and it was with incredulous surprise, and a twinge of relief, that she heard him explain he was in Denver.

"I'm waiting for a flight to New York. Something came up, and I'll be gone about a week," he continued. "Can you manage while I'm gone?"

Here was her opportunity, and she took a deep breath. "Well, I could, Cal, but it so happens, I'm not . . ."

He cut across her words, cutting her off in midsentence. "Good. I'll be sending some financial papers on a firm I'm thinking of buying. I want you to go over them carefully and let me know what you think. Take down this number where you can reach me in the event of an emergency."

Janna tried again. "Cal, I've got something to say to you, and I wish you'd listen . . ."

He interrupted her again. "Janna, I'm about to miss my plane. Whatever it is can wait." He gave her a New York City telephone number, speaking quickly and forcefully, and Janna grabbed a pencil to take it down, feeling frustrated at her inability to make him listen to her. "Have you got the number?" he asked.

"Yes," and Janna read it back to him.

"Fine. I've got to go now. See you in about a week."

Janna started to protest again, but he added another admonition. "It's very important that I get your reaction to those papers, Janna, so take care of it as soon as you get them." And then casually, "Oh, and sign that employment contract and send it to my lawyer in Cheyenne—today!"

Before Janna could say another word, he rang off, leaving her staring impotently at the dead phone in her hand. She banged it down on its hook with suppressed violence. Now what was she supposed to do? Damn Cal and his manipulating ways! She stood fuming for a moment, then went to make herself some coffee, wondering what was the best thing to do. Should she just leave as she'd planned and to the devil with his papers?

Janna indulged in some convoluted thinking for a while, the end result of which was a decision to stay a little longer—at least until Cal came back. She salved her conscience with the thought that she wasn't going to sign the employment contract after all. But deep down in the very farthest reaches of her subconscious lurked the thought that she'd reached her decision to stay because she simply didn't want to say good-bye to Cal Burke yet rather than because of any objective reasoning. At any rate, she felt a sense of reprieve as she took her coffee into the study and got back to work, and she resolutely squelched the voice in the back of her mind that whispered that she was a fool, fool, fool!

102

CHAPTER TEN

Despite Janna's determination to leave as soon as Cal came back, she couldn't help starting to work on the cottage. She simply liked the place so much she couldn't resist. She justified her actions with the thought that at least it kept her hands—and her mind—busy in the evenings. Otherwise, she'd have just sat around moping, and she'd had enough of that over Frank.

She'd made the acquaintance of two people besides Cal and Lisa now. Cal's housekeeper, Mrs. Miller, had shown up for work on the second day after he'd left town, and she and Janna had taken a liking to one another almost immediately. Mrs. Miller was a motherly older woman, who couldn't say enough about Janna's housekeeping efforts during the storm. When she learned that Janna was staying at the cottage, she brought out lengths of curtain material for inspection, and now Janna was busily cutting pretty gold material to sew up into curtains in her free time. She was thinking how nice they'd look in the living room when she heard someone at her door.

She peeked out the living room window surreptitiously and smiled when she saw Bob Willis standing there. He was Cal's foreman on the ranch and had delivered her car to her after having it repaired.

She threw open the door with a warm smile. "Hello, Bob! What brings you here this evening?"

Bob smiled shyly back at her, his eyes wandering admiringly over Janna's tousled hair and slim figure. "Just thought I'd check on you—see if you need anything," he answered in his slow, pleasant Western drawl. "It's pretty isolated out here, and you haven't been here long enough to know where to go for help."

Janna stepped back and gestured for him to come in. "You're sweet, Bob, but I'm fine. Come in and have some coffee with me, though. It'll be nice to have someone to talk to."

Bob accepted the invitation with an alacrity that made Janna smile to herself. There was no mistaking Bob's interest in her as a woman. It had been immediate and flattering. But while she liked him, she didn't return his interest in the way he would no doubt have liked. And if it hadn't been for the fact that she was leaving soon, she would have treated him more cautiously in an effort to discourage him. But as it was, what did it matter? There wouldn't be time for him to get hurt.

"How do you like your coffee, Bob?" Janna paused in the doorway to the kitchen after settling him in the living room.

"Black, Janna . . . thanks." Janna nodded and went to fix it. She left Bob sitting in the maple rocker where Cal had sat the day she'd moved in. And she was unable to resist comparing the two men . . . with Cal coming out the unqualified winner from the aspect of appeal, she thought wryly.

Bob was attractive. He had sandy hair, nice brown eyes, and a smattering of freckles across his nose. And he was as large as Cal. But there was something missing—a vitality and a presence—and the ability to create an aura of excitement. Janna thought somewhat ruefully that Bob would make someone a loving, dependable husband someday . . . but she wouldn't be that someone. In fact, she was beginning to wonder if she'd end up a spinster, and the idea was rather sobering. Still, she'd prefer it to taking less in a relationship than what Cal had shown her was possible.

Shaking her head impatiently at the direction her thoughts had taken her, Janna poured coffee and then brought it in to join Bob, determined to focus her attention on her guest instead of the absent Cal. They settled down to a leisurely chat, mostly about the storm and the cattle losses that had occurred as a result of it.

"We didn't do too badly," Bob commented. "Not as badly as some of the other ranchers anyway, the Bowers in particular."

Janna's interest was aroused. "The Bowers?" she inquired casually.

"Yes. Old Man Bower runs a spread west of here. He's getting too old to handle it, and he's too stubborn to turn the reins over to a foreman. But if Lisa has her way, I reckon Cal will be taking over their problems one of these days." Bob chuckled, unaware of Janna's tightened lips and stiff posture. "Lisa's been after Cal for years," Bob continued. "And if you ask me, she'll get him too. You've got to admire her persistence."

Janna set her cup down quickly. Her hands had started to tremble, and she didn't want Bob to notice, so she clenched them in her lap. Her brain told her to leave well enough alone, but her heart was in control, so she didn't resist the temptation to probe further.

"I wouldn't have thought any man could have resisted

105

very long if Lisa wanted him." She kept her voice calm, almost disinterested. But it required an effort. "She's very beautiful."

Bob looked at her thoughtfully as if mulling over her words. "Oh, I admit she's got the looks," he said musingly. "But underneath all that cuddly femininity, she's a pretty hard little customer. I've known her all my life, and I can tell you, I'd hate to make an enemy of her." He smiled at Janna then, his admiration embarrassingly apparent. "She can't hold a candle to you," he said softly. "Not in personality or in looks."

Janna shook her head deprecatingly and managed a smile. "Thanks, Bob. But all men aren't of the same opinion as you, you know."

"Well, I've always thought I had better sense than most," he grinned, and Janna had to laugh. "You take Cal now," Bob went on more seriously. "I respect him more than most any man I know. And he's been smart enough to stay out of Lisa's clutches so far. She even got discouraged enough to marry somebody else once. But I don't know now. Looks like he might have lost his good sense where she's concerned."

Janna was startled at Bob's mention of Lisa's marriage. "You say Lisa's been married?"

"Yup. Didn't work out, though. She came back in less than a year. Said it was all his fault, but if you knew Lisa as well as I know her . . ." Bob's eyebrows rose expressively, and he shook his head. "And now she's after Cal again."

Janna smiled faintly. "And you think she'll get him this time?"

"Can't tell yet." Bob reached in his pocket for a cigarette and offered one to Janna, who refused. She wanted

106

Bob to finish telling her his theories about Cal and Lisa's relationship, but she didn't dare prompt him too strongly. But Bob took his time in lighting his cigarette, and then Janna had to jump up to find him an ashtray. As soon as she thought she decently could, she prompted him gently.

"Why do you think Cal is weakening toward Lisa?" She affected a slightly bored expression as if she were only making conversation, but her pulses were racing.

"Well, he's been seeing a lot of her lately. At least he's been going over there pretty often. Could be he just wants to check on the old man, though. They're pretty close."

Bob changed the subject then, and Janna had to go along with it or risk seeming unduly interested. She tried to listen politely as Bob talked about the rodeos he'd entered and about the merits of different breeds of cattle and about hunting trips he'd taken, none of which interested her particularly. But she managed to throw in an appropriate question or comment from time to time, and Bob didn't seem to notice anything peculiar about her attitude, so she supposed she was hiding her feelings well enough. She was relieved when he stood up to go, however, and she didn't press him to stay.

"Say, Janna," Bob turned to her as he was about to leave, a shy expression in his soft brown eyes. "One of the reasons I came by . . ." He hesitated for a second, and then continued. "Well, the fact is there's a dance Saturday night, and I wondered if maybe you'd come with me."

Bob was shuffling his feet, and Janna felt a pang of sympathy for him. For all she knew she might be gone by Saturday night, but she felt sorry for him. There was an anxiously pleading expression on his gentle face that brought out her motherly instincts. If she were still here, why not make the effort to please him?

"Sure, Bob," she smiled at him with a friendly camaraderie. She didn't want him to expect too much since there was no question of anything permanent developing between them. "What time should I be ready?"

Bob heaved a sigh of relief and satisfaction. "About eight o'clock, Janna . . . and thanks. I didn't really think . . ." He stopped, and Janna pushed him out the door with a teasing grin.

"Oh, get along to your cows, Bob," she laughed. "And let me get along to my sewing."

"Sure thing." He was grinning all over his face. "See you Saturday, then. Bye for now."

"Good-bye, Bob." Janna gave him another smile and waved, then closed the door and leaned back against it. Instantly, her smile was replaced by a drooping mouth and sagging shoulders. So Cal was weakening toward Lisa. Well, what had she expected? That he might have been swayed by an uninvited houseguest who threw herself at him at every opportunity?

Janna choked back the tears that were tightening her throat and shrugged her shoulders in resignation. She picked up the gold curtain material and then dropped it again. What was the use in fixing up the place when she wouldn't be around to enjoy it?

CHAPTER ELEVEN

The papers Cal had mentioned arrived in the mail the next morning, and Janna spent the day sorting them out and checking figures. She was intrigued in spite of herself. The firm he was thinking of buying was a small research company engaged in experimenting with ways to use coal other than for heating. They hadn't had much success so far from what she could gather. They seemed to be concentrating mainly on economically feasible ways to produce natural gas from the coal. Janna thought the larger companies engaged in energy research probably had the edge on this small firm. They had the resources to spend so much more on research. But the books were sound, although there wasn't much chance for profit unless they came up with some spectacular new process. Their funds came mainly from royalties on coal properties the owner had turned over to the company. But it wasn't her place to make recommendations on the advisability of buying the property. She was merely to report on the reliability of their books, and they seemed in good order.

It was late afternoon before she finished, and as she put things away, she felt a sense of loneliness. Though Mrs. Miller was here today, the house still seemed empty without Cal.

Janna wandered into the kitchen to tell Mrs. Miller good-bye for the day, but the woman had left a note and was gone already. She had to attend a church function, but she'd left Janna a hot meal in the oven.

Janna smiled fondly at the unnecessary gesture. It was plain Mrs. Miller had taken a liking to her even if Cal hadn't. She sat down to eat the delicious casserole, wondering if she should call Cal to give him her report. But the decision was taken out of her hands as the phone rang.

Her heart skipped a beat when she heard the deep familiar tones of Cal's voice on the line. "Hello, honey bear," he teased softly.

"Hello, lion," Janna responded. The words were out before she thought, but she didn't regret the lapse when she heard his soft chuckle. But then he was all business, and she steeled herself against the resulting disappointment she felt.

"Did you get the papers?" he asked briskly.

"Yes, this morning," she answered cooly. "I've spent all day on them."

"Good. Then you can bring them with you when you come to pick me up tomorrow."

Janna froze. "Pick you up?"

"Yes. At the airport in Cheyenne. Be there at one o'clock tomorrow afternoon and we'll take the papers to my lawyer before we go home."

"But . . ."

"And bring that employment contract too," Cal interrupted her. "My lawyer says you haven't sent it to him yet. Is that right?" He sounded coldly annoyed . . . almost angry.

Janna's temper rose at his insistence on her signing the

110

contract, and it gave her the opportunity she was looking for.

"No, I haven't," she said firmly, "and I want to talk to you about it . . ." She got no further. Once again he was adept at cutting her off.

"Well, bring it then. I want it signed, and we can deliver it at the same time as we take in the other papers. I've got to go now." The last was said abruptly, but Janna was determined he wasn't going to put her off again.

"No, Cal, listen . . . I want . . ."

"Sorry. I'm late for an appointment. See you tomorrow." And he hung up.

Once again Janna was left holding a dead phone in her hand, and she almost threw it against the wall. She was getting good and tired of Cal Burke's uncanny ability to keep her from saying a word he didn't want to hear. And why didn't he want to hear it?

She slammed the phone down and seated herself at the table again. She'd lost her appetite, but she had to eat sometime, and it wasn't fair to dump the food in the disposal after Mrs. Miller had taken the trouble to make it.

She was washing up the dishes and still fuming to herself over Cal's behavior over the telephone when Lisa Bower walked in unexpectedly and without knocking.

"Oh! I didn't know you'd still be here." Lisa frowned fleetingly, and then cleared her brow to smile falsely at Janna.

Janna wondered how Lisa could have failed to miss her red car sitting so conspicuously out in the drive, but she merely smiled and nodded. "Hello, Miss Bower. Cal's not here if you're looking for him. He's out of town."

Without being invited in, Lisa came into the room to

111

seat herself comfortably at the kitchen table. "Oh, I know that. He called me from New York last night. I just came over to get something I left here awhile back." Lisa smiled and accepted the cup of coffee Janna offered, raising her faultless eyebrows in inquiry. "I didn't know you ate your dinner here, Miss Wilding?"

Janna stiffened. Lisa was giving a good impression of being mistress of the house. "I normally don't," she replied calmly with an effort. "But Mrs. Miller left this for me, and I couldn't turn it down. She's a marvelous cook."

"Yes, isn't she?" Lisa smiled patronizingly. "I found her for Cal, and sometimes I wish I'd kept her for myself . . . except that poor Cal would be helpless without her." Lisa sipped her coffee delicately and made a small grimace at the taste.

Janna watched her with a jaundiced eye, trying to hide her dislike. She was becoming increasingly positive that Lisa's visit had a definite purpose that had nothing to do with retrieving a forgotten article.

Lisa lit a cigarette and eyed Janna calculatingly through the drifting smoke. "How long do you plan to work for Cal, Miss Wilding?" There was an underlying contempt in her tone that set Janna's back up. She decided instantly to make things as uncomfortable for Lisa as Lisa hoped to make them for her.

"Oh, I don't know," she said with careful thoughtfulness. "He seems so pleased with my work; I imagine he'll want me around for some time yet." She returned Lisa's taut glance with one of cool blandness.

"But don't you worry about gossip?" Lisa's expression had changed to one of innocent concern.

"Gossip?" Janna raised her eyebrows in inquiry, knowing what was coming and feeling a little sick at heart about it.

"Well, after all, Cal's such an attractive man . . . and you and he were stuck out here all alone during the storm . . . and now you'll be working here together alone all day . . ." Lisa's voice trailed off and she lifted her shoulders expressively.

"Mrs. Miller can take care of any gossip that might arise, I imagine," Janna said crisply, ignoring the reference to the time she and Cal had been trapped during the storm. "She's a very good chaperone . . . if one were needed."

"Perhaps." Lisa snuffed out her cigarette. "But when Cal gets married, his wife might not appreciate a stranger in the house. He's so impetuous, it could prove awkward . . . if you know what I mean." Lisa gave a little shiver of delight and smiled wickedly at Janna.

Janna was disgusted. "Is he likely to be married soon, do you think?" she asked dryly. She waited for an answer and was surprised to see a little glimmer of uncertainty flicker in Lisa's eyes, but it was gone in an instant.

"Well, we don't want anyone to know yet . . . Oh! I shouldn't have said anything. Cal would be furious! He's such a private person!" Lisa gave Janna a look of triumph behind her assumed contriteness, and Janna felt sickened. So that's what this visit was all about! Lisa was laying down territorial lines.

"Congratulations, Miss Bower. I'm sure *you'll* be very happy." Janna emphasized the pronoun deliberately and was rewarded by a flash of malice from Lisa's dark eyes.

"I'm sure we will too," she replied coldly, making very little effort toward a pretense of friendliness now. "And now that you know the situation, don't you think it would

113

be in your own best interests to look for other employment as soon as possible?" Her face hardened into hostility. "There's really no future for you here, is there?"

"Really?" Janna kept her face expressionless. "Well, perhaps not. But I think I'll wait awhile to make plans just the same. I'm sure Cal will give me plenty of notice *if* he decides he doesn't need me."

Janna stood up and started to gather up the coffee cups to wash them. "Didn't you have something you wanted to collect while you were here?" she reminded Lisa dryly.

"Yes." Lisa's tone was abrupt. "I'll get it." She disappeared from the room and Janna sagged weakly against the sink for a moment, wondering how Cal could love a woman like Lisa. But no doubt she was completely different when she was around Cal. With a sharp pang of loss, Janna washed the cups, hoping for Cal's sake that he wouldn't regret his choice in the years to come. She was glad she wouldn't be around to know whether he did or not.

Lisa came back shortly carrying a small parcel in her hand. "I'll be going now, Miss Wilding," she said coldly. "I don't want to miss Cal's call later."

Janna nodded her head, not trusting herself to speak. Lisa turned to go out, and as she did so, she seemed to deliberately catch the parcel on the back of a chair. It fell to the floor, and a sheer negligee spilled out onto the floor.

"Oh, damn!" Lisa bent to stuff the gown back into the bag, but there was no mistaking the satisfied smirk she gave Janna in the process. "I left this here before the storm and forgot about it, I'm afraid." Her tinkling laugh jarred Janna, as she stood white-faced to watch what she knew was an act for her benefit. She was meant to draw the natural conclusions, and she did. And the resulting ache

114

of jealousy was almost unbearable. The agony prompted her to say something she would never have dreamed of seconds before.

"Are you sure it's yours, Lisa? It looks the color of one of mine that I haven't seen since I moved to the cottage. Shall we make sure?" Janna's voice was flat . . . devoid of life. But Lisa didn't seem to notice the tone—only the words, and they made her positively venomous.

"Oh, it's mine, all right, Janna," she said with a hard look in her brown eyes. "And I'd advise you to leave here before Cal has to ask you to go. It's always easier to find a new job when you have decent references, isn't it?" And with a look of pure hostility, she left the house, slamming the door behind her.

Janna slumped tiredly. Her words to Lisa had been prompted by irrational jealousy . . . and even by reckless bravery. But her emotions were left tattered and raw by the encounter with Lisa. What had she gained by bringing their mutual antipathy out into the open? And what had she lost in the process?

CHAPTER TWELVE

Janna stared longingly at Cal's lithe, tall frame as he walked toward her from the aircraft, wanting to drink in the sight of him and hold the memory for a time when she didn't have the reality. She'd never seen him in a business suit before, and the superb natural grace with which he wore it brought a lump to her throat.

She was unaware that her eyes mirrored her thoughts and her feelings as he came up to her. She was lost in the painful joy of being with him again. As he took her waist in his hands, his own eyes were crackling with a strange light that took her breath away.

"Did you miss me, honey bear?" His voice was soft, teasing . . . incredibly seductive, and Janna could only swallow and nod helplessly.

"I'm glad." He bent his dark head to brush her lips briefly with his own, and then took her arm to draw her away from the crowd heading for the terminal.

"Where's the car?" He flashed her a smile that made her heart turn over.

"Right in front," she murmured weakly, and he squeezed her arm.

"Go get in it then. I'll get my bags and join you in a minute."

He left her to join the throng at the baggage counter, and Janna hurried to the car. She had to get hold of herself, she thought desperately. What was the matter with her? Spineless idiot! She had it all planned, and she wasn't going to let herself down now . . . was she?

She was feeling fractionally more in control of her reactions by the time Cal climbed in beside her and began to direct her to the office of his attorney.

"Where are the papers?" He leaned against the door and stretched his long legs to the center of the floor to give them more room.

"In the briefcase." Janna gestured toward the backseat, and Cal leaned over to pull the case into the front seat. Janna bit her lip. She knew the first thing he would see would be the unsigned employment contract.

"Ah, you've brought the contract," he said with satisfaction. He looked at it for a moment and then shot her a sharp glance. "Why haven't you signed it, Janna?"

She didn't answer him immediately. Instead, she pulled the car over to the side of the road and parked it, then forced herself to look at him. "I'm not going to sign it, Cal."

His reaction was cold instant anger. "Why not?" His tone was harshly menacing, and the blue of his eyes had changed to fire.

"I can't." Janna turned her head away to look out the window. She couldn't do what she had to when the sight of him turned her to jelly. "I'm leaving in the morning to go back home."

"The hell you are!" Cal's hand shot out and grasped her arm to turn her to face him. "You've committed yourself to work for me, and you're going to live up to it." His hand indicated the contract. "This was to make sure you didn't

117

run out on me, but I'll damned well see that you don't whether you sign it or not!" He let go of her to thrust the contract back into the case and then threw it into the backseat.

Janna was angry in her turn now. Why couldn't he just let her go without all the fuss? If he thought he could force her into anything, he was in for a disappointment. "You can't make me work for you, Cal!" She winced as he took hold of her arm again, hurting her with his grip. "And let go of me," she cried angrily. "You're hurting me!"

"I'll do more than hurt your arm if you don't stop defying me, Janna," he said grimly, but he loosened his grip fractionally. "Why do you want to go? Tell me, damn it!"

His eyes were boring holes in her, and Janna knew it wasn't going to be easy to lie and get away with it—but she had to try. "I . . . er, I'm homesick!" She threw the falsehood at him desperately. "I want to see my parents!" She watched him fearfully to see if she were going to be believed and was not reassured by the mocking cynicism on his face.

"Ah, yes, your parents," he drawled sarcastically. "And what would your parents think if I told them you were repaying me for saving your life by leaving me in the lurch just when I need you the most. I haven't got time to find another accountant, and if you leave now, you could cost me thousands of dollars!"

Janna looked at him with sick dismay. So that was why he wanted her to stay! It was simply a matter of dollars and cents. But the threat to tell her parents hit home. Honoring an obligation was everything to her father. "You wouldn't tell my parents that, surely?" She almost whispered the words. "You can find another accountant

118

easily . . . I'm sure you can!" Cal's hard stare indicated otherwise.

"Either you sign this contract, or I call them and tell them what an ungrateful little brat they've raised. I might even ask your father for damages." His tone was implacable.

Janna was overwhelmed by the thought. Could he do that? She didn't think he could, but she wasn't sure. Well, she still had one last card of her own to play.

"Cal, listen to me." She licked her dry lips and took a deep breath. "Lisa doesn't like me. We had a . . . a disagreement while you were gone."

Cal frowned in impatient perplexity. "So what?"

Janna looked at him in bewilderment. "Well, she made it clear that once you and she . . ." Janna found it difficult to say the words.

"Once she and I what?" Cal's voice was grim, and the hard look on his face frightened Janna.

"After you're married, she doesn't want me working for you!" Janna got the words out in a rush and closed her eyes in pain, only to open them again in startled surprise as Cal grasped her shoulders and pulled her to within inches of his body.

"Get this straight, Janna!" His voice was harsh and he gave her a shake for emphasis. "*If* I decide to get married, I'll be the one to tell you, not Lisa Bower. In fact, I wouldn't be surprised if you were the first one to know. Until then, you can take it that I have no definite plans in that direction. And just to make sure you understand . . ."

Cal pulled her hard against him and kissed her mouth with a force that bruised her lips. But at her muffled exclamation of pain, he decreased the pressure . . . only he didn't let her go. Instead, he raised his head briefly and pulled her across his body so that she was half-lying in his lap, and then he proceeded to kiss her so thoroughly that she was left in no doubt that he wanted her. It was evident in the tenseness of his body, in the hungry way he took her mouth again and again—and in the way his arms tightened around her, straining to bring her ever closer to him, as if he couldn't get enough of the feel of her against him. He unbuttoned her blouse finally in rough, jerking movements that threatened to tear the material, and then he pulled her up so that he could bury his head against the softness he'd uncovered, kissing her breasts with lips that burned her skin and destroyed the last vestige of her defenses.

If it hadn't been for the blaring horn of a passing car, Janna thought he would have taken her there and then— and she knew she couldn't have stopped him. But at the sound of the horn, he drew back shudderingly, running his hand down the length of her body and looking into her eyes with a possessive desire that sent a shaft of fire through her veins.

He lifted her away from him reluctantly, gently, and then bent to rest his elbows on his knees, supporting his head with his hands. He stayed like that until his breath slowed, and by the time he looked up, Janna had her blouse buttoned and had straightened her skirt, but her eyes were still softly bemused. He smiled at her crookedly and reached over to run a finger over her lips, seemingly pleased at their swollen fullness, and at the fact that he'd made them that way.

"It's a good thing we're out here in a traffic jam, Janna," he said softly. "Otherwise, you'd have lost your innocence for all time—you know that, don't you?"

Janna nodded, her eyes telling him she wouldn't have cared. Her look made him open his own eyes wider, and he fixed her in that smoldering blue fire. "Will you stay with me tonight, then? You've played hell with my control long enough, I think. It's time we picked a time and a place where we won't have to worry about being interrupted." His husky invitation was spoken so softly and temptingly that Janna had to strain to hear. But hear, she did. Every heart-stopping word.

She stared at him for a long moment before she said the word she'd had in her heart from the first moment he'd touched her. "Yes." She said it simply, lovingly and irrevocably. And she meant it.

He smiled slowly at her then—a charming, twisted movement that expressed a promise Janna took to her heart. And for the first time, Janna let herself hope that Cal might love her. She was going to belong to him—and there was a chance he might become hers along the way.

Their visit to the lawyer's office was brief. Janna explained her findings regarding the financial papers, and after a short, general discussion she and Cal stood up to leave. And then Cal pulled out the employment contract and handed it to Janna with an intimate, teasing look on his face that took the sting out of the gesture for her. His expression seemed to say that he wanted her to sign it more to seal their bargain to become lovers rather than regard it as a business contract. She felt a small qualm even so, but as his eyes darkened with the familiar possessiveness that always brought a surge of longing to her senses, she shrugged off her misgivings. She was committed to him in her own mind, so what did it matter if she transferred that commitment to paper?

When she straightened up from signing the document and looked at Cal, he silently communicated his satisfaction at her action by flashing her a look that promised so much to come that Janna was glad she had decided to please him in the matter. He handed the papers to his attorney, and after they said their good-byes, he took her arm and they left the room and the building with Janna feeling as if she were drifting on a cloud of anticipation.

The ride home held a dreamlike quality for her that she was always to remember. They said very little, but Cal pulled her close to him so that she sat with her head on his shoulder with his hand resting on her knee. She didn't think consciously about what was to happen once they reached his home. Rather, she seemed to drift in suspended animation, aware only of the inner contentment she felt at resting against him in relaxed harmony, watching the strong brown hand guide the car with sure skill. The rough texture of his coat under her cheek, the smell of his shaving lotion, and the smooth hardness of his jawline made up her world for the time being, and she was happy. It was enough.

She bestirred herself and sat up only as they neared the lane to the house, thinking she wouldn't want Mrs. Miller to see them like this if the woman were still there and hadn't left for home. She was of another generation and wouldn't understand. And the thought of the motherly woman's probable condemnation of what Janna was about to do brought the first chill into the dream world Janna had been living in for the past couple of hours. Was it a matter of being of another generation? she thought a little sadly. Were morals a cultural thing to be juggled according to the times—or were they timeless? She'd always considered them to be the latter until now. But then she hadn't known Cal before now—and he had the power to sweep everything else from her mind—common sense, her own pride . . . her self-respect?

The second, far more deadly, chill came when she saw Lisa Bower run out of the house as Cal pulled the car to a stop. She heard his muffled "damn!" and turned to see him running a frustrated hand over his dark hair. But when Lisa came up to the car, his features reflected only pleasure at the sight of her.

"Cal, darling! Whatever took you so long? I've been waiting for what seems like hours!" Lisa trilled the words with a breathless laughter and a warmth in her eyes that enhanced her attractiveness—and she was looking her best in a white suit that set off her dark coloring and feminine curves. Janna looked down at her own disheveled appearance in wry resignation. But when Cal got out of the car and Lisa pulled his head down to her own to give him a long, lingering kiss, Janna stiffened and forgot appearances. Cal didn't seem to be resisting the embrace. To the contrary, when he finally lifted his head, he was laughing as if delighted at the welcome. Lisa put her arm around his waist and pulled him along with her toward the house, and he didn't resist that either. It was if he'd forgotten Janna existed!

Janna watched them with a suffocating pain that grew with every step the two of them took away from her. There was no room for even the humiliation she knew she should be feeling in the face of Cal's betrayal. That would come later. Now her only thought was that she had to get away before she broke down completely under the agony that filled her heart and mind to the exclusion of all else. She slid numbly under the wheel of the car, turned on the ignition, and threw the gear lever into reverse with such

123

force that there was a grinding noise of protest. Then she was backing down the lane to the road to turn the car into the direction of the cottage, calculating with desperate urgency how long it would take her to pack and be on her way. She heard Cal shout her name as she narrowly missed hitting the post with the rural mailbox at the juncture of the two roads, but that only spurred her to press harder on the accelerator so that the car fairly leaped along the dirt road, skidding dangerously in the loose dirt. She brought it under control and continued on her way.

She covered the mile to the cottage in record time and screeched to a stop with jolting suddenness. Then she flung open the door and ran to the house as if the devil were on her heels, heading straight for the bedroom.

As she pulled out her suitcases, jumbled thoughts cascaded through her brain. How could she have been such a fool as to have believed Cal felt anything for her other than a purely animalistic attraction? Lisa had spelled it all out, and still she had fallen for his lies about not having any plans for marriage. And she'd signed that contract on the strength of his word!

She was cramming clothes into the bags with little regard for neatness when she heard the door to the cottage open. She froze instantly, knowing before his powerful frame filled the doorway to her bedroom that it was Cal. They stood staring at one another for long seconds, and then his eyes took in the half-packed cases and Janna's defiant stance and his face hardened into grim determination. "What do you think you're doing, Janna?"

His words triggered sheer rage in Janna. What did he think she would be doing in the light of what had just happened? Waiting patiently until he could find the time to continue his hole-in-the-corner affair with her?

"What does it look like? I'm leaving!" Janna faced him squarely, her brown eyes shooting sparks of challenge, her tone daring him to try to stop her.

"You're going nowhere," he said flatly. He took a step into the room, and Janna involuntarily stepped back at the sight of the hard purpose in his ice cold blue eyes.

"You can't stop me, Cal," she almost shouted at him, trying to make him see the strength of her conviction by raising her voice. "I don't ever want to see you again, much less work for you!" She clenched her fists, her whole body taut with tension. "Now get out of here and let me pack in peace!"

It was with utter astonishment that she saw him suddenly relax and open his seductive, traitorous mouth in a pleased chuckle. But after the first moment of stiff surprise, the pain that had been forced into the back of her mind by anger washed over her in waves almost too agonizing to be borne. "Oh, God!" The words were forced out of her by the strength of her battered emotions, and tears gathered in her eyes before she could stop them. She turned her back to him so he wouldn't see what he could do to her and desperately tried to control the sobs that threatened to break out at any moment.

"Janna . . ." Cal crossed the room to stand behind her and took her shaking shoulders into his hands. "Janna . . ." he breathed her name again, his mouth against her hair. "Are you jealous, Janna . . . of Lisa?" His voice was caressingly tender. But there was still a thin thread of amusement in it that tightened her already shattered nerves.

Janna couldn't answer him. Instead she tried to pull away, but at her movement, he moved his arms to her waist, imprisoning her in a steel band she had no hope of breaking, and he drew her back against his chest so that she could feel his breath stirring her hair.

"Didn't you listen to me this afternoon?" His voice was rough, all traces of amusement gone. "I told you I have no plans for marriage right now."

"No, I'm sure you don't," Janna said huskily through her tears. "You just like to take what you want from as many women as possible, don't you?" She shook her head weakly in self-contempt. "And I was ready to become one of those women—but not any longer."

"I can't deny that I'd like to take what I want from *you,* Janna." Cal's voice was husky, and Janna was dismayed at the shiver of warmth that shot through her at his words. She could feel the tension of desire gathering in his body, and it brought an echoing, traitorous response in hers in spite of her resolve and her self-disgust at her weakness. He almost completed the destruction of her purpose by leaning down to kiss the side of her neck at the same time as he moved his hand to her midriff under her blouse, stroking her with hard, warm, disturbing fingers.

"Stop it!" Janna struggled against him, determined he wasn't going to win this argument the same way he'd won the last one they'd had. But he wouldn't let her go. He turned her roughly to face him, and she felt the full impact of his body against hers.

"Janna, don't fight me! I can't explain about Lisa right now . . ."

"What's there to explain?" Janna half-laughed, half-sobbed the words as she pushed against his chest. "It's perfectly obvious what's going on between you two, and it means nothing to me . . . nothing! Do you hear?"

But Janna couldn't hide her tears, and Cal wrapped her closer against him. "I'm afraid I don't believe you, little honey bear." His voice held no hint of mockery, and there was no mistaking the tenderness in his tone. "Shall I show you why I don't believe you?"

Janna raised moist eyes to his, their brown depths filled with pain and the awful, pride-destroying wish to believe in him again. And the moment her eyes found his, she was locked in a swirling, dizzying maelstrom of hope. His blue gaze held more than desire—although that was there too —but it was mixed with such tender and loving . . . yes, loving! . . . regard that all her resolutions to stand firm against his attraction were washed away in the echoing response of her whole body to what she saw there.

"Cal . . ." His name was a sigh of returned love and surrender, and he took advantage of her capitulation without hesitation, bending his dark head swiftly to kiss her parted mouth.

In the quiet privacy of Janna's bedroom, the dam broke between them, and all the passion they'd felt earlier returned, redoubled in force. Janna opened her heart and her body to him as if they already belonged to him, returning kiss for kiss, softening to the molding of his hands and demands until all that separated them were the clothes they wore. It was very clear that Cal wasn't intending to let anything stop him from removing even that barrier this time. He pushed her to the bed without releasing her mouth, and Janna felt her knees buckle against the mattress. In an instant she was lying on her back with the hard length of Cal's body pinning her down, and her blood was soaring at the feel of him against her. As he began the final stages of her seduction, skillfully, tenderly, his hands and mouth created havoc wherever they touched her. She moaned his name and raised a hand to unfasten his shirt, wanting the warmth of his skin against her. He wanted the same, and he copied her action, raising himself on one elbow to look at what was revealed as if he couldn't see enough.

"Now?" Cal said the word more as a statement than a question, and Janna could only nod weakly as his hands moved to the button of her skirt. Her heart was singing with the rightness of sharing with Cal this most intimate of moments, and she was raising her arms to pull him down to her when her name was called.

"Janna, are you home?" It was Bob's voice at the door, and the sound of it was like a cold douche of water over Janna. Instinctively, she jerked away from Cal and looked at the door of her bedroom.

"Keep still!" Cal's whisper was rough, angry with frustration, and he kept her where she was. "He'll go away in a moment if you don't answer."

"No . . ." Janna felt as if she were coming out of a dream. "Let me up, Cal. He can see both of our cars out front, and if I don't answer, he'll think . . ." Janna bit her lip.

"I don't give a damn what he thinks!" Cal's voice was hoarse, and he lowered his head to brush a kiss on her bare shoulder. Janna shuddered with renewed desire, and Cal smiled sensuously. "We've waited long enough, Janna. I don't want it spoiled this time," he whispered softly.

"Janna?" Bob was calling again, and Janna reluctantly struggled to sit up.

"Please, Cal. He's not going away. He may think something's wrong and try to get in to check."

"Oh, hell!" Cal sounded violently disgusted, and the frustration in his voice found an echo in Janna's mind, but as he let go of her, she sat up, fumbling at the buttons of her blouse.

"You don't have to tell him I'm here if you're afraid of what he'll think," Cal's voice was hard. "I rode over with one of my men—my car's not out there." He leaned back, hands behind his head and watched her straighten her clothes with eyes that glittered with hunger.

Janna flashed him a startled glance, wondering fleetingly if it were Cal who didn't want anyone to know he was here . . . someone like Lisa Bower, for instance. But she didn't have time to mull over the thought as she hurried to the door, closing it behind her, and continued on to the front door. It was with mingled annoyance and guilt that she threw it open to see Bob halfway down the steps. He'd evidently given up hope of being acknowledged, and Janna felt a brief flash of real anger as she realized that Cal had been right. He would have gone away if she'd stayed quiet!

"Janna! I was afraid something was wrong when you didn't answer." Bob came back up the steps, and as he saw Janna's tousled appearance, a concerned and puzzled look replaced the pleasant relief he'd displayed at first. "Are you all right? You're not sick, are you?"

Janna flushed uncomfortably. "No . . . no. I'm all right, Bob. I was . . . er, I was taking a nap." She hated the lie even as she said it and felt guilty as chagrin flashed over Bob's features.

"And I woke you up!" He sounded disgusted with himself.

Janna smiled faintly. "Don't worry about it, Bob. Er . . . what did you want to see me about?" She hoped fervently his reason for coming was not just to chat. She didn't think she could stand making small talk in the living room while Cal waited in the bedroom . . . the sordidness of a scene like that made her feel cheap.

129

"I just wanted to remind you that I'll be picking you up around eight tonight."

For a moment Janna's mind was completely blank—what was he talking about? And then as she remembered about the dance she'd promised to go to with him, she felt dismayed. She'd forgotten all about it!

Hoping he hadn't noticed her reaction, she smiled hesitantly at him. "Oh, of course, Bob . . . eight o'clock, you say?" How could she get out of it?

"Right." Bob looked relieved. "And we'll be going with Cal and Lisa. No sense taking two cars when we're all so close."

"Cal and Lisa?" Janna repeated the words with a cold sense of inevitability.

"Yeah, they always go together." Bob was looking at her suddenly pale face with concern. "But are you sure you're all right? You don't look well."

Even as her mind reeled with the news, a grim determination filled Janna with cold purpose. "I've said I'm fine, Bob!" She almost snapped the words at him, and then she took pity on him as she saw how hurt he looked. "I'll be ready at eight . . . which doesn't leave me much time to get ready as it's six now." This with a quick look at her watch.

"Sure . . . sure. I'll be on my way then." Bob turned to go and then looked back at her. "And Janna?" He smiled shyly at her. "Thanks for coming with me."

He sounded so grateful and pleased that a dart of shame penetrated Janna's preoccupation with how she was going to approach Cal with this new development. She smiled warmly at Bob in unconscious penitence.

"My pleasure, Bob. See you later." She gave a weak little wave of her hand in response to Bob's happy grin and then turned back into the house as he moved jauntily off to climb into his pickup truck.

Janna closed the door and stood with her back against it, eyes closed, trying to sort out her thoughts.

"So you're going to the dance with Bob?" Cal spoke to her from the doorway to the bedroom, and Janna's eyes flew open. She couldn't see his eyes—he was lighting a cigarette, which was unusual for him—he very rarely smoked. And his question had sounded as if he were angry.

"Yes, I am." She kept her voice firmly under control. "And I understand we're to go with you and Lisa." She allowed a faint note of contempt to inject itself into her tone.

At that his head came up with a jerk. Narrowing his eyes calculatingly, he studied her with an alert consideration. "Is that so?" He drawled the words, but his eyes belied the casual tone. "And when did these arrangements take place?"

"You tell me," she retorted. "After all, I wasn't there when you made them."

He strode across to her and grasped her arms with biting hands. "No . . . I mean when did Bob invite you? And when did you accept?"

Janna tried to pull away, but he held on to her. "That's none of your business," she snapped.

"Isn't it?" Cal tightened his grip. "Everything you do is my business, and you know it." He gave her a rough shake. "When, Janna?"

"Oh, what difference does it make! I haven't asked you when you invited Lisa, have I?"

He shook her again. "No, but if you had, you'd have found out I didn't invite her. It's just become a tradition that I take her. To tell you the truth, I'd forgotten all about it!"

Cal's words mollified her in some strange way, but she wasn't about to give in to his arrogant demand that she account to him for her actions. He was still taking Lisa regardless of how the arrangements had been made. "Well, I don't have to tell you anything about Bob and me—and I don't intend to!"

For a moment Cal's grip tightened so much that he hurt her. But as he studied her face, he slowly relaxed and a lazy smile quirked his lips. "Well, never mind, then, honey bear . . . I think I can guess."

Janna flung away from him, incensed at his attitude. The trouble was he had every reason to be conceited where she was concerned. Hadn't she melted every time he'd come near her?

Cal walked slowly and arrogantly to the door. "See you tonight, Janna." There was a look of male satisfaction in his blue eyes that infuriated her.

"Yes, Bob and I are looking forward to it," she said, sweetly sarcastic. "As I'm sure you and Lisa are."

At that, Cal laughed deep in his throat and went out the door. He didn't reply, but went off whistling a cheerful tune off-key, leaving Janna staring after him in frustrated disbelief. She had the uncomfortable sensation that she hadn't fooled him one bit in trying to make him just as jealous of Bob as she was of Lisa—except at first. If he hadn't been jealous when he'd first learned she was attending the dance with Bob, he had certainly given a good imitation of it.

The thought lifted her spirits, and she went off to dress feeling better than she'd believed would be possible when she was going to get ready for an evening out with Cal Burke and Lisa Bower . . . and then Cal had left her rather than finish what had begun earlier in the bedroom. Lisa had managed indirectly to come between them once again.

CHAPTER THIRTEEN

Janna studied her reflection in the mirror with a critical eye. She wanted to look her best, and she was gratified at the results of her efforts. The halter-necked dress in a delicate beige flattered her coloring, and as it hugged her body to the waist and then flared out into a full-length skirt, it did wonders for her figure as well. Gold accessories completed the ensemble, and Janna thought the elegant simplicity of her outfit was very sophisticated.

Now she gave a last-minute inspection to her hair and makeup. She had washed her hair and fluffed it into a windblown, honey-streaked aureole around her face, and she did think it looked rather glorious! A soft, golden eyeshadow over her warm brown eyes, and a touch of pink blush to her cheeks and on her lips, and she was amazed at the effect of a young, healthy, sensuously attractive young woman that stared back at her. All in all, she thought she'd never looked better and could pass the most rigorous inspection. The only trouble was Cal was a master at the art—and Lisa Bower had had a lot more practice in satisfying his tastes, and she had the money to enhance her natural beauty with the best in clothes, make-up, and accessories.

Shrugging her shoulders irritably at the thought of competing with another woman, Janna picked up a bottle of perfume to add the final touch. She'd never indulged in the game of trying to outdo another woman in vying for the attention of a man. If the man didn't like her as she was, then so be it! And she didn't want to start now, even for such a man as Cal. But on this occasion, she needed the reassurance of looking her best—and she thought she'd accomplished that.

Janna gave herself one last fleeting look in the mirror and then grabbed a cobwebby shawl to place around her shoulders. She would wear her brown velvet evening cape to and from the dance, but the shawl would serve to keep her bare shoulders warm once they got there.

A knock sounded on the front door as she left the bedroom, and Janna congratulated herself on her timing as she crossed the room to let Bob in. The look they exchanged after half-uttered greetings was almost identical—and it was one of pure and simple shock!

"Janna!" Bob was recovering slightly, and as his eyes traveled over the lovely picture she presented, the shock was replaced by unmitigated admiration. "Honey, I'm sorry . . . I thought you knew this was a barn dance. We don't dress up much for them . . ." Bob looked down at his jeans and plaid shirt deprecatingly, and his tone was apologetic. "Not that you don't look beautiful!"

Bob's sincerity was apparent, but it was also apparent to Janna that he was embarrassed by her failure to dress properly for the occasion . . . and she was embarrassed, too, to say the least!

Her mortification increased a thousandfold when Cal strolled up to join Bob at the door. "What's the problem?" he asked, and then as he took in Janna's appearance, he burst out laughing!

Janna was stunned! Here she'd worked on her appearance for two solid hours, and the man she most wanted to approve of her efforts was laughing at them! Hard on the heels of her immediate disappointment came a stubborn anger born of pride and nerves rubbed raw by the perverse machinations of the man who stood in front of her managing to look as suave and exciting in faded dungarees and red flannel shirt as he had in a business suit earlier that day. Janna didn't know what was customary for women to wear to a barn dance, but even if she'd had the perfect garment, she wouldn't have put it on now! And if Bob didn't want to take her in what she had on, that was just too bad!

Ignoring the sardonic gleam in Cal's eyes as he controlled his laughter, Janna tossed her long, beautiful hair, shrugged her shoulders prettily, and looked at Bob, giving him a brilliant smile. "Sorry, Bob," she said lightly and flirtatiously. "This is all I have to wear. If you'd rather not take me . . . ?"

"Not take you?" Bob protested heartily. "Why, Janna, I'd be proud to take you anywhere even if you weren't wearing a stitch!" And then he blushed in confusion at what he'd said, while Cal eyed him with a cynical amusement tinged with . . . what? Arrogant challenge? Janna didn't know, and she didn't care . . . at least not at the moment.

She gave a tinkling laugh and flashed Bob an impudent glance from her sparkling eyes. "Why, thank you, Bob—I appreciate the sentiment, but I think I'm well enough covered, don't you? Let me get my cape, and we can be on our way."

Janna held her head high and swept down to the waiting car with Bob hurrying along beside her, a protective hand on her elbow. Cal was already back in the car, and he didn't get out as Bob opened the rear door for Janna. It was only as she ducked her head to get in that she saw Lisa seated in the front seat beside Cal and knew at once that the other woman was enjoying the situation enormously.

"Why, Janna," her laughter tinkled falsely. "Whatever possessed you to put on that thing for a barn dance?" She made it sound as if "that thing" were a potato sack instead of a fairly expensive and very lovely evening gown, but Janna stopped the sharp reply that hovered on her lips. Instead, she forced a smile onto her stiff lips and managed to answer quite airily and cheerfully.

"Oh, I'm afraid I haven't been here long enough to acquire a suitable wardrobe for this type of function." She paused, and then with sudden inspiration, she tacked on innocently, "Give me a year or so, and I ought to be ready for anything."

She saw Lisa stiffen and smiled unhappily to herself. Her little barb had accomplished two purposes—she had hit Lisa where it hurt with the implication that she, Janna, would be around for quite some time . . . and she had allayed any suspicions Cal might have that she still contemplated leaving here. For Janna hadn't shelved the idea by a long shot. She knew without a shade of doubt that Cal Burke could make her his mistress anytime he felt like it—and he knew it too. And the idea was beginning to frighten her to the core of her being. She'd always pitied women who allowed themselves to be used by men with no thought for the future. But here she was, so susceptible to Cal's touch that every sensible thought went right out of her head. Seeing him with Lisa this afternoon—and now, watching them from her position in the backseat— Janna thought despairingly that if she didn't leave soon, she might never be able to. And that could mean a lifetime of living in the shadows, with no self-respect, no home and family—nothing, in fact, but the dubious ecstasy of short moments in his company. The prospect was appalling!

As the ride to the dance progressed, Janna was grateful that her remark to Lisa had the effect of silencing the other woman's poison tongue. Lisa reserved her conversation strictly for Cal, ignoring Janna and Bob. And while Janna was inwardly miserable at the fact that Cal, too, seemed to have forgotten her existence, she managed to keep up a facade of interest as Bob chatted to her.

By the time they reached the huge barn where the dance was to be held—and Janna was surprised to see that it actually *was* a barn—all of her enthusiasm, if she'd ever had any, for the evening ahead had drained away. She dreaded facing the critical eyes of countless strangers when they saw how she was dressed—she dreaded having to keep up an appearance of enjoyment for Bob's sake—and most of all, she dreaded seeing Lisa in Cal's arms again while they danced.

It was all she could do to force herself to take Bob's hand and step out of the car, but once out she straightened her shoulders and fastened a smile onto her trembling lips, preparing to face whatever came with as much composure as she could muster.

Once inside the door to the barn, the expected barrage of eyes turned to examine the newcomers, stopping on Janna with interest and surprise. Janna was gratified to find that the men's surprise turned quickly to admiration —but some of the women pursed their lips in censure, and the fact depressed her still more. Somehow she got through several introductions without faltering, and finally the crowd lost interest in her as the music started and

138

couples drifted onto the floor to form squares for square dancing, Cal and Lisa among them.

Janna fortunately had learned square dancing in a class at college, and she enjoyed it. But she didn't look forward to renewing her acquaintance with it under the present circumstances. Bob, however, upon learning that she did, in fact, know the dance, pulled her into a square with three other couples, and Janna had little choice except to comply gracefully.

The other couples were young, and the brunette girl across from Bob seemed to be sympathetic to Janna's discomfort; at least, she gave her a quick smile of friendliness. And then the fiddles started, and the caller began his litany so that Janna had to concentrate on his words.

"Allemande left and do-si-do, swing your partners to and fro!"

Bob was an enthusiastic partner, and as Janna moved in and out among the flounced skirts of the other women and the blue-jeaned legs of the men to be caught and twirled around again and again, she began to lose some of her embarrassment and inhibition in the spirited movements of the dance. She was almost breathless after two or three rounds—square dancing was rigorously strenuous!—but she felt much better emotionally than she had. Still, she was grateful when Bob laughingly declined an invitation to make up another square when the first dance came to an end. She felt in need of a drink, and he escorted her to a refreshment table with alacrity, his arm resting almost possessively around her slender waist. Janna would have pulled away, but as they came toward the table, she caught sight of Cal and Lisa standing near it talking to a dignified elderly gentleman, and she let Bob's arm stay where it was. If Cal did have any inclination to be jealous, she thought it was high time he had a taste of how painful it could be.

"Janna . . . Bob." Cal dipped his head casually as they came up, his blue eyes frosting slightly when he saw Bob's arm around Janna's waist. Lisa looked almost pleased, however, and Janna thought sourly that it was too bad one couldn't have one pleasure without suffering a loss at the same time.

"Janna, I'd like you to meet Lisa's father, Mr. Zeke Bower. Zeke, this is Janna Wilding, my . . . er, my accountant." Janna noticed Cal's hesitation over the explanation of her status and felt a sharp stab of pain at his prevarication. But, after all, that's what she was officially, wasn't it? It was only unofficially that she was a candidate to be his mistress as well.

Hiding her pain as best she could, she looked up into two faded, but sharply perceptive brown eyes that were taking her in with an encompassing sweep that gave her the sensation that she had no secrets from this white-haired, kindly gentleman. She had expected to dislike Lisa's father on sight, but instead she found herself charmed by his courtly bow and his obvious pleasure at meeting her.

"I'm happy to meet you, Miss Wilding," he said quietly. His manners were charming, and his tone was completely sincere. Janna found herself responding to his warmth.

"Hello, Mr. Bower." Janna impulsively offered her hand, and to her delight, the elderly man took it and carried it to his lips instead of shaking it. He really was a dear!

From the corner of her eye, Janna caught Lisa's scowl of displeasure at the rapport that had been so quickly established between her father and Janna. But Janna didn't care, and as she turned to accept a glass of cold lemonade from Bob, she gave Mr. Bower a smile of sincere appreciation as she withdrew her hand from his.

The talk was casual for a few moments, and then the musicians began a lovely waltz. To Janna's surprise, Mr. Bower offered her his arm.

"You don't mind if I steal your girl for this one, do you, Bob?" The faded brown eyes twinkled at her, and Janna smiled up at the handsome old gentleman warmly and took the arm he offered. He didn't give Bob a chance to say whether he minded or not—and in any case, Janna had effectively stopped any protest Bob might have made by accepting the offer on her own—and she thought fleetingly that in some ways the elderly man could have been an older replica of Cal with his arrogant overriding of any anticipated interference in his plans. But he was infinitely safer than Cal—and much more soothing to cater to. So she turned into his arms willingly, feeling almost light-hearted . . . until she caught sight of Cal's tall figure escorting Lisa onto the dance floor.

The sudden pang of jealousy that swept through her almost made her stumble as Mr. Bower swept her into the first steps of the waltz, and she saw him looking at her with a disconcerting awareness in the soft brown of his kindly eyes. But he said nothing, and as he guided her around the floor, Janna had to concentrate on following him—he was an excellent dancer and not shy at all about his capabilities! In spite of the raggedness of her emotional state, she began to enjoy his expertise as he swung her around in wide arcs, making her skirt fly out around her ankles.

Janna had always enjoyed dancing and was quite good at it. As Mr. Bower began to appreciate her potential and enthusiasm, he let go of any restraint he might have been exercising and soon they were the focus of all eyes as he twirled her around the floor. One by one the other couples dropped back to watch, until Janna and the elderly Mr. Bower had the floor to themselves. It was a marvelous experience, and secure in his arms, Janna smiled back at the unmasked appreciation in his eyes, her own echoing his pleasure.

She felt a sense of regret as the music finally faded and their steps slowed, then came to a halt in the very center of the floor. Their performance was rewarded with a spontaneous burst of applause from the spectators that brought a flush of pink to Janna's cheeks and a bow of acknowledgment from Mr. Bower. His face creased in a smile of pure pleasure, he escorted her to where Bob, Cal, and Lisa waited. Janna couldn't resist a quick look at Cal to see his reaction, but she couldn't read his expression, and as he bent his head to say something to Lisa, she quickly turned her attention to Bob. His expression at least was all she could have wished for, and he caught her by the waist and twirled her around in an excess of exuberant spirit.

"You were great, Janna! And you, too, Mr. Bower." Bob grinned happily at Janna and gave a respectful nod to the older man.

Mr. Bower smiled benignly. "It's always easy to look good when you've got a beautiful woman on your arm, young man . . . but I think you already know that." He spoke rather dryly, taking in the fatuous look on Bob's clean, decent face as the younger man looked at Janna.

"You always did like to draw attention to yourself, Father." Lisa spoke pettishly and gave her father an impatient look, and then her glance settled on Janna and a flash of hostility replaced the impatience. "You really shouldn't

142

encourage Father in things like this, Janna. It may give you a chance to show off, but it's not good for him. He has a heart condition!"

Janna drew in her breath sharply at the criticism and then she looked at Mr. Bower in dismay. She hadn't known about his heart or she would never have consented to dance with him! She was alarmed at the unhealthy color that had suffused his face. But the color seemed to be the result of anger at his daughter rather than from the exertion of dancing, as was borne out by his words.

"Lisa, I'd appreciate it if you'd keep that sharp little tongue of yours quiet long enough for me to enjoy this evening. My health is all right as long as I don't lose my temper, but you don't seem overly inclined to worry much about that!" There was an uncomfortable silence after he'd delivered himself of the rebuke, and with quiet dignity, the elderly man turned his back on his furious daughter and went to join a crowd of friends his own age where he soon relaxed and assumed his cheerful demeanor once again.

Janna stood awkwardly for a moment, unable to think of any way to relieve the uncomfortable silence. Lisa looked ready to explode. Cal had a thoughtful expression on his face as he watched Lisa glower at her father's back, and Bob just looked rather amused as he winked at Janna behind Lisa's back.

"Come on, Janna. Let's take our drinks to that corner over there. I see a couple of empty seats, and I haven't had you alone all night." Bob handed her a glass and took her arm to pull her in the direction he'd pointed out. Janna risked one last look at Lisa . . . and wished she hadn't—the other woman's hostility had switched from her father to Janna—and then one last look at Cal, and the same feeling applied. For Cal was scowling now with clenched jaw, and his blue eyes were as cold as ice as they swept across Bob and Janna and lingered on Bob's hand where it clutched Janna's arm possessively.

Janna looked quickly away from him and smiled rather wanly at Bob as he pulled her along away from the others. She wasn't sure what had set Cal off, but he looked positively dangerous, and it was just as well to get out of his way while he was in that mood!

Once settled in the chairs Bob had indicated, Janna raised her glass to her mouth and took a small sip, then eyed the contents suspiciously. It was apple cider! She debated about drinking the rest of it—it was hot in the room, and she was thirsty—and finally, she shrugged her shoulders and finished it off. It was only one glass after all. She'd had much more than that the day she and Cal had made love on the bear skin rug. This was just enough to give her a warm glow. And she needed that glow after what she'd been through today—and after being reminded of what had happened the last time she'd had apple cider! Gripping the glass tightly in her hand, she tried to shut her mind to the pictures that memory brought to the surface. Bob was chatting away beside her, but she heard scarcely a word as she scanned the crowd for the one man she wanted to see, almost without realizing what she was doing.

She found him at last. He was alone, and he was coming toward where she and Bob sat. Janna watched the graceful movement of his tall, powerful body with unconscious longing, and then her gaze traveled up to the rugged face to find Cal's blue eyes fixed on her with possessive intent.

She supposed she'd been in love with him all along, but it was not until that moment that the positive recognition hit with such clear force that it rocked her where she sat.

The room and Bob's voice faded away until there was only Cal in her world. She knew her thoughts and feelings were mirrored plainly in her eyes as Cal came up to her, but she couldn't hide them for the moment. They were too new and too powerful.

Cal stood silently for a moment, studying her face with intent regard. Then he smiled a peculiar, tender smile and held out his hand to her. He pulled her to her feet and into his arms as the slow, sweet strains of a modern ballad echoed from the strings of the fiddlers' instruments. And Janna came into the circle of his arms as if she belonged there. She could feel the warmth of his body through his clothes as he pulled her close to him, and she rested her head against his chest, savoring with every nerve the feel of her hand in his, the beat of his heart, and the lean strength of his arm around her waist.

They danced in silence, with perfect accord, seeming to have created an intimacy of their own that shut out the crowd and left them alone to enjoy their harmony. Janna was so lost in the illusion that when Cal lowered his head and whispered in her ear, she had to struggle to comprehend his words.

"We'll be leaving here in a few minutes, little honey bear. Don't take too long in saying good night to Bob, will you? I'll be over after I've taken Lisa home."

Janna raised her head reluctantly as the last strains of the music died away in concert with his words. Cal held her to him for a moment after the music stopped before he let her go to look at her with possessive eyes that raked her face and flicked briefly over her shoulders, finishing at the deep vee of her bodice. And then he turned her back toward where Bob sat waiting and escorted her back to him. Janna's legs felt weak, but she managed to cross the room, vibrantly aware of the touch of Cal's hand on her elbow. It was only as she heard him ask Bob if he were ready to leave that the full implication of his words made themselves felt in her brain. Was he coming to claim her finally . . . irrevocably . . . and without the love in his heart that she felt for him? And could she resist him even so?

Janna tried to gather her thoughts as the four of them left the building and then drove to her cottage. But it was no use. She was still locked in a daze of discovery, and she couldn't get much past reiterating over and over again in her own mind that she loved Cal! How could she have been so blind to that fact and attributed her reactions to him as simply physical attraction?

As Cal stopped in front of the cottage, Janna came out of her daze enough to murmur a quiet good night to Lisa, who ignored her, and then to Cal, who nodded to her and gave her a quick, meaningful smile. And then Bob was accompanying her to her door, and she was hoping somewhat distractedly that he wouldn't try to kiss her good night. The moon was bright, and Cal could see every move they made. Besides—there was only one man's kisses she wanted . . . even though kisses and physical love were probably all he was prepared to share with her.

But, apparently, Bob was determined to have his reward for the evening. He didn't ask, nor did he give any warning at all. He simply grasped her shoulders and kissed her hard on the mouth before she could muster her defenses. And Janna felt nothing but irritation. Here was a man who would probably be willing to share all of his life with her in time—and yet she couldn't respond.

"Janna, can I see you again soon?" Bob had dropped his hands from her shoulders when it became obvious that

Janna wasn't pleased with the embrace, but he didn't seem to be ready to give up his pursuit.

"I . . . I . . ." Janna didn't know what to say. Now was not the time to get into a long, involved discussion with Bob, and it would be too cruel to give him a flat no.

"I'll call you tomorrow, shall I?" Without giving her an opportunity to respond, he moved to the steps and started down.

"Bob . . ." Janna stood hesitantly, not really having any words to refuse him.

"I'll call you, Janna," Bob called to her and then opened the rear door of Cal's car to climb in.

So Janna gave him a half-hearted wave and went into the cottage to try to make sense of her troubled emotions. She simply had to have a plan of action for when Cal came back. Discovering that she loved him made that imperative!

CHAPTER FOURTEEN

An hour passed before Janna heard Cal's car returning. And by that time, she was angry. So he'd wanted her to say good night to Bob quickly, had he? Well, it was plain he'd felt no need to do the same where Lisa was concerned! The anger gave her the strength and the purpose she badly needed to carry out her plan. Cal Burke was not for her. Instead of weakening toward what she was sure would be another attempt to seduce her, her love for him had shown her at last that she was not prepared to spend her life waiting in corners for what small crumbs of his time he was prepared to give her. Better to say good-bye now than to submit to him and then find she was trapped in a love that would leave her nothing but shame.

She sat quietly as she heard his step on the porch and then his knock on the door.

"Come in . . . it's open!" Janna's voice was clear and firm, and she stayed where she was in the maple rocking chair as Cal came through the door.

"You really should lock your door, Janna," he drawled laconically as he came to stand in front of her, his hands in his pockets, his whole attitude lazy and casual. "You never know who might decide to pay an unexpected visit." His blue eyes twinkled at her even as they raked her body.

Janna raised her eyebrows and gave him a cool look. "Yes, I suppose I should. Manners do seem to be more casual out here than back home." She paused and decided to give herself time to catch her breath before telling him she was leaving. "Would you like some coffee?"

The invitation came out stiff and prim, and it was Cal's turn to raise his eyebrows. "I think not." His voice was low, determined and provocative. "I didn't come here for coffee, Janna."

Janna stiffened and felt the urge to get up and move away. But he was standing directly in front of her. "Why did you come, Cal?" She tried to sound casual . . . discouraging even. But her voice broke in the middle, and her hands clenched the arms of the rocking chair tightly.

"Come here and I'll show you." Cal leaned forward and grasped her shoulders to draw her up to him.

"No!" Janna's voice was strangled, and she was inwardly cursing her stupidity in binding herself to the chair with no room to maneuver. Cal's hands were burning her skin, creating within her the insane desire to let him have his way.

"Yes, little honey bear." Cal's tone was sensuous and determined, and he exerted pressure to jerk her up to him ruthlessly.

"Cal, don't . . . please!" Janna struggled against him, but he held her firmly with one strong arm while he forced her face up to his with the other.

"This has been a long time coming, Janna," he murmured against her mouth. "I'm not waiting any longer to make you mine."

Janna tried to avoid his mouth, but his lips captured hers relentlessly, and at his touch she felt the old weakness invading her limbs. In desperation she fought harder

149

. . . against herself as well as him. But Cal was like a rock, and her struggles only succeeded in making him kiss her so hard that her lips were bruised under the pressure of his. And finally it became too hard to fight the desire he created so effortlessly. As he felt the response of her body, Cal softened his kiss to a mere whisper of tender, seductive temptation that made her ache with longing for more. He moved his lips to her neck and down to her shoulders, grasping her hips to keep her hard against him, tantalizing her with his mouth so skillfully that her hands came to his head to press him against her. A moan escaped her as he caught her mouth again, and she opened her own to allow him to take his fill of the warm softness within.

Cal's hands moved to her neck to untie the knot of her halter top, and then her breasts were free to his touch, and Janna was on fire with desire. She pressed her lips against his neck, moaning his name over and over. It wasn't until Cal's lovemaking took on a fierce inevitability that made Janna aware he was losing control that her dazed senses regained some clarity. In another second, he would have her in the bedroom . . . he was pushing her there slowly, almost imperceptibly. And beneath the drugging passion he had created in her, the thought took hold that once she had succumbed, she would truly be lost. He could do anything he liked with her after that, and she wouldn't be able to escape his domination.

It took every ounce of her will to drag her mouth from his and raise her arms to push against his chest. "Cal, no . . . !" Her voice was weak, but contained a purpose that made him look at her. That in itself was almost her undoing. The blue of his eyes was clouded with passion and longing.

"God, Janna, don't say that! You're mine! Don't you

know that yet?" He crushed her to him, and Janna knew she wasn't going to be able to stop him with her feeble struggles. She had only words left as weapons, and she had to use them.

"I'm going back to Frank, Cal!" She flung the words at him desperately and was rewarded by the instant stillness of his body. He reached up to grasp her shoulders roughly and hold her away from him, his eyes fierce as they looked at her.

"What did you say?" He was dangerously quiet, but his eyes were blazing with anger—so much so that Janna felt afraid of him.

"I said I'm going back to Frank," she said weakly, closing her own eyes against the look in his.

"The hell you are! You told me he was married to your friend!" Cal shook her roughly, and Janna steadied herself by grasping his elbows.

"I . . . I lied!" Janna's deception was confusing her. "At least, I thought he would have married her by now—but he called me today and said it was all off. So I'm going back."

Janna looked up at him anxiously, willing him to believe her. But he was suddenly smiling! Her reaction was one of complete bewilderment as he moved his hands down to her waist to hold her lightly.

"Is that so?" He was almost laughing at her. "And your parents . . . are they pleased?" He drawled the question, and Janna felt still more confused and on her guard.

"Oh, yes . . . yes, of course." Janna stared at Cal as he shook his head, a smile quirking his sensuous mouth.

"Funny," Cal watched her closely. "When I talked to your father this evening, he asked me to tell you Frank and his wife were expecting a baby. Don't you think he might have been a little concerned at the thought of you breaking up their happy home?" Cal watched the stupefied amazement spread across Janna's face with satisfaction. "Oh, yes, Janna . . . your father and I have gotten to be quite good friends since I pulled you out of that car."

Janna's knees almost buckled as Cal suddenly let go of her and moved to sit down on the couch, thrusting out his long legs in complete relaxation.

She finally found her voice. "You're crazy! You've never spoken to my father in your life!"

Cal's eyebrows rose as he eyed her mockingly. "Haven't I? Are you sure of that?"

"But . . . but . . ." Janna sputtered in her confused dismay.

"Tut, tut, girl. Can't you find the words?" In Janna's eyes Cal seemed to be enjoying himself. But there was still a suggestion of watchful alertness about him that made her somewhat cautious.

"All right," she snapped. "When did you and my father get to be such close friends?"

Her sarcasm went unnoticed. "Since I called him to tell him you were all right, and that I'd rescued you from certain death." There was a smug gleam in his eyes as he saw Janna's reaction to his self-glorification. "He was most grateful to me," Cal continued. "Pity his daughter can't show the same gratitude."

"Oh, shut up!" Janna was angry again. How dare he sneak around behind her back and keep in touch with her father—why had he done it? "He's never mentioned to me that you and he were on such good terms. Why is that?"

Cal's eyes narrowed. "Careful, Janna. There are worse fates than freezing to death in a car, and if you don't keep a watch on your tongue, I might be inclined to show you one or two of them." Then his features relaxed back into a smile. "As a matter of courtesy, I talked to your father to let him know you're safe and doing well. What's wrong with that?"

"Safe . . . with you?" Janna bit her lip, regretting her spontaneous outburst instantly. But Cal's eyes mocked her.

"Yes, safe. What's the matter, Janna? Do you have trouble believing that?"

Janna shrugged her shoulder impatiently, avoiding his eyes. "I wasn't too safe a few moments ago, was I?" She muttered the words, unable to resist saying them, but half-hoping he wouldn't hear her.

"Ah, but you've never wanted to be safe with me in that way, have you little honey bear?" Cal's voice was low, suggestive . . . and still mocking.

Janna flushed at the tone, but she couldn't deny that he was right. She faced him finally. Now was her chance.

"I do now, Cal." She spoke firmly, willing him to accept her wishes. "I'd like you to leave. And I'd like you to accept my resignation."

Cal's reaction was instant and immovable. "No on both counts, Janna. We have some things to discuss, and we're going to do it now!"

Janna looked at him in helpless frustration, wondering what it would take to reconcile him to letting her go— short of the truth!

"Since we've exploded the myth of your going back to be with Frank, I suggest you tell me why you found it necessary to invent such an excuse in the first place," Cal continued, leaning forward and fixing her in an intent gaze. "Why are you suddenly intent on leaving again? I thought we had that all settled."

153

Short of telling him it was as simple as having finally faced the fact that she was desperately in love with him and not prepared to share him with Lisa Bower, Janna had no reply that would hold water, so she turned sharply away and went to the window. She was afraid her eyes would give away her reasons.

"You don't have to have a reason, do you?" Her voice was trembling. "Maybe it's just that I don't want you for a . . . a lover . . . and I want to get away from the loneliness out here."

Cal came up behind her silently and circled her waist with his arms. "You want me, all right, Janna. And you've shown every indication of liking it out here. So you'll have to do better than that, I'm afraid." He nuzzled her ear, and Janna trembled at his touch. She realized with a sense of despair that she was going to have to drag her pride in the dust in order to win free of this man. Perhaps in this case the truth really was the only thing that would set her free. Cal surely didn't want that kind of complication upsetting his planned arrangements.

Janna swallowed convulsively as Cal's hand stroked her waist and then moved to her stomach to press her back against him. "Cal, I love you!"

She hadn't meant to say it like that, but he was playing havoc with her senses again, and the words burst out in pure defense. And she didn't know quite what she'd expected his reaction to be, but certainly not what it turned out to be.

After a barely perceptible pause, he continued to stroke her stomach. "You're sure you're over Frank, then?" He spoke quietly.

"I've been over Frank for a long time," she replied, equally quietly. "Almost from the day I met you."

154

Cal sighed. "Are you sure? You're not just falling for me on the rebound?"

Janna's eyes opened wide. Was that what he thought? She turned to face him. "I was on my way to recovery when I left home, Cal. And since I've met you, I haven't thought about Frank. You've had almost my every thought, and all of my emotions." She spoke softly and sincerely, and Cal's eyes were penetrating as he watched her face.

"If I could only believe that." He was pulling her closer to him as he spoke, and Janna had all she could do to stop him.

"But there's always Lisa, Cal. I can't stay here and watch you and her . . ." She stopped, unable to put the thought into words. "Surely you understand?" She dipped her head to hide the tears that were forming, but he lifted her head to look into her eyes, and his were tender as he wiped away a tear with a thumb.

"Forget Lisa. You'll understand about her one of these days. For now, this is all you need to think about." He lowered his head to kiss her, taking her lips gently, tenderly, coaxing her to respond. And, of course, she did. He hadn't really explained anything, but her resistance was nonexistent when confronted with this new side of Cal's wooing. She could believe he cared for her when he was like this.

And when his lips became more demanding, it was already too late for her to wrap herself in the protection of what pride she had left. His hands asked, and her body affirmed, melting into the hard contours of his as if the two of them had been molded to fit together in an intimacy only they could share.

Cal lifted her in his arms and started for the bedroom,

155

and Janna lay against his chest quiescent and defeated, allowing his domination of her without equivocation. He paused at the door and gave a low laugh of triumph and then kissed her with hard possessiveness. "From this moment, you belong to me body and soul, Janna. Don't ever forget it."

"Yes, Cal . . ." With heart pounding, Janna breathed the words of her capitulation and then caught his head to make him kiss her again. All her reservations were gone. She was committed to this enigmatic and yet totally exciting man with all her heart. And she was his to do with as he pleased.

Janna was almost expecting the knock on her front door when it came. It seemed she and Cal just weren't destined to share the ultimate intimacy. She dropped her head against his chest and would have giggled in near hysteria —wondering if she had a guardian angel whose job it was to keep her pure—but Cal's reaction was anything but humorous. He swore with a vehemence that stifled Janna's laughter. Then he lowered her to the floor almost violently and gave her a push into the bedroom.

"Stay in here, Janna. I'll get rid of whoever it is. This is one time when nothing is going to stop me!"

Janna glanced at the clock as Cal strode to the door. It was two o'clock in the morning! Who on earth would be coming here at this hour? Her nerves jerked as she heard Bob's voice when Cal flung open the door.

"Cal!" Bob sounded shaken and belligerent rolled into one, and Janna flinched as she realized the interpretation he would place on Cal's being here at this hour. And it didn't help at all that his interpretation would be the correct one.

"What the hell do you want, Bob?" Cal's tone was

156

harsh as he challenged his employee. Bob looked over Cal's shoulder to where Janna stood framed in the bedroom door, hair tousled and cheeks flushed, and his expression was grim.

"Well?" Cal's impatience and hostility were evident, and Bob's answer was sullen when it came.

"Lisa sent me to find you."

"Lisa!" Cal thundered the word, and Janna stiffened in cold resentment.

"Old Mr. Bower has had a heart attack. The doctor's there now, and Lisa wants you to come right away." Bob explained his mission in a taut, angry voice that didn't soften as he saw the change in Cal's attitude and Janna's white face behind him.

Cal hesitated only a second, turning to Janna with a drawn look replacing the anger he'd displayed before. Then facing Bob again, he spoke quietly. "I'll go right away. Thanks, Bob."

Bob gave the two of them a surly, contemptuous look and left the porch to return to his truck and drive away. Cal shut the door behind him and took Janna's hands in his own.

"I've got to go, darling. Do you understand?" He was looking her straight in the eyes, his own pleading with her as much as Cal Burke was capable of pleading with anyone. Janna nodded. She felt as let down and miserable as she'd ever felt in her life. Once again Lisa Bower was separating them—although she could understand why under the circumstances—and on top of that she felt guilty about her dance with Mr. Bower earlier in the evening. Had that caused this attack?

"I'll call you as soon as I know anything. Or come by when I'm able to leave the Bowers." He pulled her against

157

him and kissed her hungrily. "God, Janna, we haven't had any luck at all in getting together, have we?" He kissed her again, more gently this time. "But we will—I promise you that." And his mouth hardened in determination, then relaxed into a rueful smile. "If I have to take you to a desert island to make love to you in peace, I'll do it. Remember that!"

He was gone so quickly, Janna hardly had time to whisper good-bye. And it was a long time before she crossed to the bedroom to get undressed and climb into her lonely bed to lie dry-eyed for hours. It was only as she was drifting into sleep that she realized Cal had called her "darling" for the first time. If only it wouldn't be the last.

CHAPTER FIFTEEN

Janna slept badly, tormented by dreams of Cal and Lisa together and then of old Mr. Bower dancing with her again only to clutch his chest and fall to the ground. In her dream she was bending over him, begging him to be all right, when a loud clap of thunder woke her to a gray, rainy dawn. She lay still for a moment, reliving the events of the previous evening. Cal hadn't telephoned, nor had he come back. So she assumed Mr. Bower's condition was truly serious.

Reluctantly, she dragged herself from the bed, knowing she couldn't go back to sleep, but feeling as tired as if she hadn't slept at all. She banged her toe into a suitcase at the side of the bed, and the pain was a vivid reminder of her futile plan to leave here. Well, she couldn't go now, she thought dully. She might not have a real chance with Cal, but if there were any chance at all . . . He had told her not to worry about Lisa. But that could mean lots of things besides what Janna would like for it to mean.

She was sitting at the kitchen table, wondering if she should call to inquire about Mr. Bower—she was very worried about him—when the telephone solved her question. Thinking it must be Cal, she ran to pick up the receiver. "Hello?"

"Janna? Bob here." Janna's heart sank. Not only was she disappointed that it wasn't Cal, but Bob's voice held a quality almost of contempt that raised her hackles. Consequently, she was somewhat abrupt with him.

"Yes, Bob. What is it?"

"Cal wants you over at the Bowers right away, so you'd better hop to it." There was no mistaking the sneer in Bob's tone. But Janna was too startled to take note of it.

"The Bowers? But why? Has anything happened . . . ?" Mr. Bower hasn't . . . ?" She stopped, feeling an almost unbearable weight of guilt and sadness. If only she hadn't danced with him . . .

"No, no, he's still alive." Bob relented somewhat in his tone. "He's going to require a lot of care though, and he and Lisa count on Cal's help. So I guess he'll be spending most of his time over there from now on." The sneer was back now, but Janna refused to be baited.

"I don't know how to get there, Bob. Can you give me directions?" She spoke crisply, not wanting to endure any more of Bob's contempt than she had to.

"Oh, I'll be taking you. Be ready in thirty minutes." He hung up the phone before Janna could protest. Having to face Bob's diminished opinion of her was the last thing she needed at the moment. But since there was nothing she could do about it, she went to dress as quickly as she could.

Twenty minutes later, she was choking down a piece of toast she didn't want, deliberately blanking her mind to why Cal wanted her at the Bowers. She would assume it was to help until she knew differently.

Bob came to fetch her moments later, and his cold contempt was altogether different than the half-adoring respect he'd given her a scant few hours earlier. Janna

160

flushed as his eyes raked her from head to toe with disrespectful intensity. She had pulled on the first thing that came to hand, and she was now wishing her jeans weren't quite so tight nor her red sweater quite so clinging.

"Are you ready?" She kept her tone cool and her eyes the same as Bob leaned against the door inspecting her. A mocking smile curved his mouth.

"Oh, I'm always ready," he drawled suggestively. "And now that I know you are too, maybe we can get together sometime. Unless my boss has his exclusive brand on you?"

Anger and disgust flooded through Janna with an intensity she'd seldom felt before. So much for her judgment of what a sweet fellow Bob was. Even if she deserved such treatment—and she didn't feel that she did—she'd never approved of a double standard that said a man could have his fun, but a woman who did so was a tramp. She knew she shouldn't bother to reply in kind, but she wanted to hit out at this hypocrite.

"As a matter of fact, Cal does have his brand on me. And it's the only brand I've ever had or am ever likely to want. I happen to be in love with him. So I think you'd better forget any ideas you may have been getting along that line, Bob. Now may we go?"

Her words angered Bob, she could tell, but as she watched, he damped the anger down, and his reply surprised her with its sincerity.

"You're a fool, Janna. Don't you care that Cal's only using you? He's probably going to marry Lisa, and you're only someone to play around with. You're too good for that!"

Janna stared at him wordlessly, hating him for stating her own fears openly. He crossed the room and took her hands, all his earlier contempt gone in his obvious concern for her.

"Don't throw yourself away like this, Janna. Cal's always been able to do what he liked with women. I hoped you were different. I'd hoped you and I . . ." He stopped when he saw the withdrawal in her eyes. "Well, hell, Janna. I was only trying to make you see sense. But I guess Cal's gotten to you like he has to every other woman he's ever wanted." His tone was bitter, and he turned toward the door impatiently. "Let's go, then. We don't want to keep him waiting," he said sarcastically.

Janna wanted to say something to acknowledge his concern for her, but she felt too dead inside to form the words. So she merely pulled on her raincoat and followed him silently to his truck.

The rain came down steadily as they drove along the country road, and Janna stared through the dripping windshield without seeing the country or the cattle all around them. Bob's words had hurt because she was so afraid they were true. Her own instincts had been telling her much the same thing all along. And instead of driving toward Cal, she should be running in the opposite direction. But she had to know about Mr. Bower first. She felt responsible for his condition. And if there were anything she could do to help, she would. Only when that dear old man was out of danger could she consider what was best to do for herself.

Bob slowed the truck to make a turn onto a dirt road leading to an old-fashioned house with a wide veranda on three sides. He slewed around in the mud, but straightened the vehicle with unconcerned expertise and speeded on to come to a stop in front of the old house. Cal's car was parked to one side, and Janna's nerves tightened at the sight.

She climbed down to follow Bob to the veranda, and as they came up the steps, the door was flung open and Cal came out to meet them. Janna looked at his tired face and felt a quiver of tender concern for him. He smiled briefly at her and then gave Bob instructions to relay to Mr. Bower's ranch hands. Bob nodded, and with one last glance at Janna, he left her to Cal, who took her arm and led her into the house. Once inside, he drew her into a study, the principal features of which were a stone fireplace topped by an antelope's head. There was a cheerful fire in the fireplace to chase away the chill brought by the spring rain.

Cal shut the door and pulled her into his arms to give her a soft kiss of welcome. "I'm glad you're here, honey bear," he murmured tiredly a moment later. Then he pushed her away from him gently and crossed the room to where a tray of coffee stood on a table in front of the fireplace to fill two cups.

Janna followed him and sat down on the brown leather sofa. "How is Mr. Bower?" she asked softly, and Cal ran a tired hand around his neck.

"Holding his own so far. But it was a bad attack, and he's not out of danger yet." Cal seated himself beside her. "I hated to ask you to come, Janna. I know how you feel about Lisa." He paused as Janna stiffened involuntarily. "But the fact is, we need you here."

Janna heard the plural pronoun with a sense of inevitability. She kept her eyes down as she replied. "I'll be glad to help Mr. Bower in any way I can, Cal. I feel responsible for what's happened to him . . ." She stopped as Cal broke in in puzzlement.

163

"You responsible? How could you be responsible, Janna?"

"I danced with him last night." It seemed a million years ago now. "And Lisa said . . ."

Cal made an impatient sound. "Forget what Lisa said. Zeke has had a heart condition for years. And he's as stubborn as a mule. Dancing with you gave him more pleasure than he's had in a long time, believe me. And no one can stop him when he makes up his mind about something. So there's no need to blame yourself." He stood up and paced the room restlessly.

"I might as well put you in the picture. Zeke will need a lot of attention. We're hiring a nurse, but he gets crotchety with most strangers. And Lisa . . . well, he and Lisa have their difficulties."

Janna noted the "we" again, and the fact that Cal was reluctant to condemn Lisa's inability to get along with her father even in these circumstances. Her spirits sank even lower as she waited for Cal to continue.

"It seemed to me that you and Zeke got along fairly well last night, and I thought maybe . . ." Cal paused, and Janna sat straighter in the face of the inevitable. She liked Zeke Bower, and in spite of Cal's reassurances, she still felt a certain amount of responsibility for his current condition.

"I'll be glad to help Mr. Bower, Cal. Just tell me what you want me to do."

Cal smiled at her then, and her heart turned over at the charm of it. "I knew I could count on you, Janna. It'll probably just be a matter of relieving the nurse and sitting with him for a while everyday. Let's just take it as it comes."

Janna nodded agreement, and Cal came to stand in

front of her. He was starting to bend toward her when there was a sound at the door, and he moved away. He was standing at the fireplace when the door opened to admit Lisa.

"Oh!" Lisa stopped stock still when she saw Janna, and a frown marred the beauty of her rather wan face. "What are you doing here?" Lisa hadn't seen Cal yet, and her question was couched in a waspish tone that was anything but welcoming.

Janna looked at Cal, who strolled to Lisa's side. Lisa turned startled eyes to him. "Oh, Cal, darling, don't tell me you're going to work at a time like this?" Lisa grasped his arm and turned soulful, teary eyes up to him.

"No, Lisa," Cal said gently and patted her hand where it lay on his arm. "Janna's here to help you and your father."

Lisa flashed Janna an impatiently hostile look. "But we don't need her. I can get someone from town to come out." There was a pettish tone to her voice that made Janna tighten her lips in disgust.

"So you can," Cal soothed her matter-of-factly. "But you know that Zeke won't have anyone around him unless he likes them . . . and he seemed to take a liking to Janna."

Lisa glared at this. "Too much so! If he hadn't made a fool of himself dancing with her, he might not be in his present condition!"

"Lisa!" Cal's voice was harsh and held a warning that made Lisa subside. Janna knew the woman was too smart to challenge Cal openly when he used that tone. "I think you'll find Janna will be a big help," Cal went on calmly. "Having her here will keep you from becoming totally strung up and exhausted while Zeke is confined to his bed." Cal was gently pushing Lisa toward the door now, but Janna didn't miss the sudden calculating expression that came and went in a second in Lisa's rather cold brown eyes.

"Well, it'll give me more time to spend with you anyway, darling." Lisa flashed Janna a spiteful look as she said this before allowing Cal to guide her out of the room. Cal sent Janna a cool, warning look that did nothing to ease the tight band of hurt anger that was building up in her chest. So she was to serve as the means to allow Cal and Lisa time together while Zeke Bower was ill?

As the door closed on the two of them, Janna sprang up to go to the window and stare out, helpless frustration making her tremble. Did he expect her to stay here under these circumstances? He knew how she felt about him. Was he so hard that he expected her to put aside her own feelings in the matter?

She bowed her head, fighting the tears. But then Cal had never said he loved her. Only that he wanted her. And she knew he was ruthless enough to take what he wanted . . . without regard for whom he hurt.

The door opening behind her made her swing around, brushing the tears out of her eyes with a trembling hand. Cal took in her set, drawn features, his own reflecting his weariness, and yet determination as well.

"Mr. Bower wants to see you." The words cut across Janna's preoccupation with her own problems. "Come upstairs. I'll show you to his room."

Janna didn't move for a moment, and Cal shut the door behind him. "If you're thinking of running away again, Janna, then don't! That old man needs you. I think once you've seen him, you'll realize how much."

Janna stared at him, feeling ashamed and resentful at the same time. "Mr. Bower hardly knows me," she said tightly. "Why should my presence mean anything to him one way or the other?"

Cal leaned back against the door and crossed his arms against his chest, his eyes penetratingly intent. "Some people don't take long to make up their minds about who they care about . . . and what they want from those they do care for. Mr. Bower's one of them." He straightened up suddenly and put a hand on the doorknob. "Now come on. He's waiting."

Janna had to give in. Apart from Cal's persuasions, there was still the matter of her own guilt over Mr. Bower's illness—and the fact that she genuinely liked him and was concerned about him. She crossed the room and passed Cal to enter the hall outside, and he followed her and then took the lead up a wide staircase to the second floor. Janna swept an admiring glance at the polished mahogany railing that followed the red-carpeted stairs to the upper landing. This house was old, but it had a charming atmosphere that would have made it attractive even without the expensive decorations.

As Cal stopped outside a closed door, Janna directed her attention to what awaited her on the other side of it with considerable anxiety. After a last, meaningful look at her, Cal pushed the door open to reveal an old-fashioned, unmistakably masculine bedroom dominated by an enormous four-poster bed in dark mahogany. In the center of the bed lay the frail form of Zeke Bower, his white hair forming a frame for his drawn, pale face. He opened his eyes at their approach, and Janna could see that while he was undoubtedly weak, his spirit remained unconquered.

She smiled spontaneously and went to the side of the bed, her self-consciousness forgotten at the sight of the welcoming, though weakened, smile he gave her. "Hello,

Mr. Bower," she said softly, trying to keep her eyes from showing the alarm she felt at his wan appearance.

"Hello, my dear. It's kind of you to come. I promise not to keep you long." His voice was quavery, and Janna's heart contracted with pity at his condition and at his assumption that she wouldn't want to stay near him long.

"You keep me as long as you like, Mr. Bower," she reassured him firmly, unconsciously reaching for his hand. "I don't want to tire you, but nothing would give me more pleasure than to keep you company."

Janna meant what she said, surprising herself even at the sincerity of her feelings, and the old man seemed to sense the genuineness of her words, for he smiled up at her with gratitude and pleasure. "Thank you," he said simply. "Perhaps if you wouldn't mind sitting with me awhile . . . ?"

"Of course." Janna looked around for a chair, only to find Cal was already bringing one to the bedside. As he put it down, his blue eyes caught hers in a brief glance that expressed his own gratitude at her action, and for a moment they shared a mutual concern over the man in the bed, albeit silently. Then Janna dropped her gaze and concentrated on Mr. Bower.

To keep him from talking in his weakened condition, she began to talk, saying the first thing that came to mind, complimenting him sincerely on the beauty of his home.

She heard Cal leave the room quietly, but she resisted the temptation to look up. Instead, she continued to talk softly to Mr. Bower until he fell asleep finally, a peaceful relaxation on his lined face. But he still had hold of her hand, and Janna was afraid to withdraw it for fear of waking him. Besides, she dreaded leaving the sanctuary of this quiet, peaceful room and having to face the emotional turmoil of seeing Cal and Lisa together again.

As she looked down at the wrinkled, but dignified face of the elderly man in the bed, she knew she was somehow committed to helping here until he was better, even if the circumstances were likely to involve her in a great deal of personal anguish. What did it matter if she were being used for purposes other than what was apparent on the surface. She must just concentrate on the pitiful figure in front of her. For some reason Mr. Bower had taken to her strongly. He had visibly relaxed under the soothing sound of her voice and was already looking better than he had when she had first entered the room. She had to stay until he was well enough not to need her. She resolutely closed her mind to what would happen after he recovered.

The quietness of the room, coupled with the fact that Janna had had very little sleep the night before, combined to make her drowsy and lethargic. Before long, her head was somehow on the bed beside the gnarled old hand that clutched her own even in sleep, and her mind went mercifully blank as slumber wrapped her in the peace of forgetfulness. She didn't know how long she slept, or what woke her finally. But all at once, she was wide awake. As she raised her head, groaning softly at the stiffness produced in her neck and back by her unnatural position, she saw what had caused her to wake. Cal stood in the doorway watching her, a peculiar tenderness in his eyes and smile. Then he shifted his gaze to the patient, and Janna realized Mr. Bower was awake. He still had hold of her hand, but he let it go as she straightened up fully, and the familiar twinkle was evident in his faded brown eyes as he exchanged a smile with Cal.

"There was a time when beautiful young women didn't

fall asleep in my company, Cal," he joked feebly. "I guess I truly am old."

"Oh, I'm sorry!" Janna's cheeks reddened in embarrassment at her lapse, but Mr. Bower waved a weak hand in deprecation of her apology.

"Think nothing of it," he said gently, and then his eyes twinkled again. "But I tell you, Janna, if I were a few years younger and a whole lot stronger, I'd have been tempted to take advantage of your little sleep. You have no idea how pretty you looked." He chuckled feebly at her reaction.

Janna had reddened even more at his teasing, and she darted a quick glance at Cal. "I can't think what's the matter with me," she said somewhat jerkily, for Cal's look had told her plainly that he concurred heartily in the older man's sentiments.

"Never mind, Janna. The nurse is here." He moved into the room to stand at the foot of the bed and addressed Mr. Bower. "Do you want to meet her now or wait awhile?"

The old man frowned at the news, and then looked rather anxiously at Janna. "You won't leave because she's here, will you, Janna? You're so good for me, my dear."

Janna hastened to reassure him, feeling a pang of helplessness at this evidence of how quickly he had come to depend on her. She was already too fond of him herself to even try to extricate herself from the bonds of his affection.

"I'll be here as long as you want me, Mr. Bower." She reached over and patted his hand. "Don't worry about it, please."

The man relaxed and smiled up at her. "Thank you, Janna . . . thank you." He sounded very weak now, and Janna eyed him with concern. Then the sound of voices reached her from the hallway outside. A moment later

Lisa Bower swept into the room with a large, pleasant-faced, middle-aged nurse in tow. Lisa ignored Janna and came to stand beside Cal, linking her arm through his.

"How are you, Father?" Without giving him time to respond, she turned quickly to the nurse who had moved to the side of the bed on her own initiative and was inspecting her patient with a practiced eye.

"This is Mrs. Monroe, Father. She'll be looking after you." Lisa flicked an unfriendly glance at Janna finally, acknowledging her presence in typical animosity.

Mr. Bower looked up at Mrs. Monroe, his heavy white eyebrows twitching mutinously. "I don't need a nurse," he said defiantly, but the quaver in his voice told a different story. "Janna's going to look after me."

There was an awkward silence as Mrs. Monroe's eyebrows rose in query to Lisa. Lisa shot Janna a look of unveiled impatience and hostility, and Janna gave first Mr. Bower and then Cal a look of startled dismay.

"But I'm not a nurse, Mr. Bower." Janna tried to conciliate him. "I'll be glad to stay with you, but there are things I don't know about. I won't be much use to you except as company. You need Mrs. Monroe too."

Lisa opened her mouth to say something, and it was obvious from her expression that whatever she was about to say would be highly uncomplimentary to Janna, when Cal smoothly interposed himself into the conversation.

"Janna's right, Zeke. You need both of them. After all, they'll each need a break from time to time."

The old man looked suspiciously at Cal first, and then at Janna's concerned expression, and finally at Mrs. Monroe's amused tolerance. Then he gave in. "Well, I suppose you're right, Cal," he said reluctantly. And then he laid down the law. "But you'd better learn my ways

171

fast, young woman," he said to the middle-aged Mrs. Monroe. "Or I'll send you packing, don't think I won't!"

Mrs. Monroe merely chuckled and reached down to take his pulse. Then she frowned and looked at the others. "I think Mr. Bower had better rest now," she said pleasantly but firmly. And it was obvious that she was concerned about her patient's condition. Indeed, Zeke Bower was looking exhausted.

Lisa started to protest, but Cal drew her firmly to the door. "Right, Mrs. Monroe. It's time for lunch anyway." He gave Janna a speaking glance, and she hurriedly moved to follow him.

"You'll be back later, won't you, Janna?" Mr. Bower's weak plea stopped her, and she turned to give him a brilliant smile.

"You bet! Just as soon as you've rested," she said in a cheerful voice designed to reassure him. And he seemed satisfied by that reassurance, his eyes closing wearily as Mrs. Monroe moved quickly to fetch his medicine.

Janna followed Lisa and Cal out of the room, only to hesitate outside the closed door, reluctant to follow the two of them downstairs. Cal looked over his shoulder and saw her, drawing Lisa to a stop.

"Come along, Janna. Lunch is ready." And Janna did as she was told, however much she hated every step of the way.

CHAPTER SIXTEEN

The large oak dining room table could have seated twelve, and Janna felt a little odd as Cal sat down at the head of the table and Lisa sat to his right. That left a place setting to his left for Janna. She took her seat, wondering if she should place any significance on the fact that Cal had automatically taken the place of honor at the head of the table. Was it simply that he was a male eating with two women, or was it his natural arrogance, or something more?

The door to the kitchen opened and a small, energetic woman with very dark eyes came bustling in to place salads in front of them. "How's Zeke?" she addressed Lisa familiarly as she placed a salad in front of her. Her tone was more that of a relative than a servant, and Janna watched curiously to see how Lisa would respond.

"Oh, he seems all right," Lisa said pettishly, her lovely mouth drawn into a pout. "The nurse is with him now. You might take her up a tray in a while, Mattie."

The woman addressed as Mattie nodded and then fixed Janna with an unfathomable look. "What about this one," she said somewhat discourteously. "Is she staying? I'll need to fix up a room for her, if she is."

Cal intercepted Lisa's inhospitable glare and addressed

Mattie himself. "Yes, she's staying, Mattie," he said firmly. "Fix her up with a room close to Zeke's if you can. She's going to be helping out with him."

Mattie nodded, but Janna thought the woman's face expressed almost as much displeasure as Lisa's did. However, she made no comment and disappeared into the kitchen again.

Silence reigned at the table as the three of them started their meal, and just as Janna thought she couldn't take another minute of it, Cal finished his salad and leaned back to wait for the next course. "I'll run you over to the cottage to get some clothes after lunch, Janna," he said casually, causing Lisa to look up with sudden interest.

"There's no need for you to do that, Cal," she smiled at him sweetly. "I'll take Janna." Janna shrank from the idea of a ride to the cottage and back with this woman and prayed Cal would say something to prevent it. She felt sure the offer was made to enable Lisa to warn her off again. It was with relief that she learned Cal was determined to have his own way.

"No, I have to stop by my house and get some papers anyway, Lisa," he said imperturbably, but his tone brooked no argument. "And you need to help Mattie get the rooms ready for the nurse and Janna, don't you?" He said it more like a statement than a question, and Lisa subsided impotently while her eyes expressed volumes as she stared at Janna across the table.

At that point, Mattie returned with plates of roast beef and new potatoes, and further discussion was effectively stopped. The food was delicious, but Janna had to choke her portion down. She didn't know how long she was going to be able to take staying in this house with Lisa's hatred palpitating in the very air. Only the thought of the defenseless old man upstairs strengthened her resolve enough to allow her to put aside her own acute discomfort. Thinking of Mr. Bower's need for her was the only way she would survive the next days or weeks.

The seemingly interminable meal ended at last, and Cal stood up. "Get your coat, Janna. There's still a nip in the air, and I believe it's still raining."

Janna left the two of them together, grateful for a respite, however brief, before she had to be alone with Cal. She collected her raincoat from the hall closet and then stood stiffly at the front door, waiting for Cal.

He came almost immediately, and they went to the car without speaking to one another. The rain had slowed to a miserable drizzle, and Janna gazed around at the gently rolling country, trying hard not to notice that Cal's leg was so close to hers. She could almost feel the heat of it, and she could smell the after shave he used, although it was mixed with the soft scent of early spring wild flowers that dotted the countryside. Spring was coming to the Wyoming countryside, and it was hard to believe that only a short time ago, the whole area had been blanketed in snow—a snow that had destined that her already battered heart would be tested to the limits by one Cal Burke.

Janna was wrapped in her own thoughts when Cal pulled the car to a stop in a layby and lit a cigarette. She looked at him warily. Why was he stopping? Surely he didn't intend to make any advances here, she thought somewhat disgustedly, but at the same time, she knew the treacherous excitement of expectation.

As the silence dragged on, her nerves tightened. "Why have you stopped, Cal?" Janna forced herself to sound calm, but she didn't feel it.

Cal cocked a dark eyebrow at her, and she noticed again

the lines of weariness around his blue eyes. "I wanted to rest a moment," he said simply, and his voice betrayed his tired state. Janna felt ashamed of her suspicions, and a little disappointed too.

"And we have to talk," Cal continued.

Instantly, Janna was alert and wary. "Oh?" She struggled to sound casual, but her heart had started to beat so fast, she was afraid Cal could hear it.

"Yes," he answered quietly. "The next few weeks are going to be pure hell, Janna. I'm sorry it has to be this way, but things don't always work out the way we'd like."

He paused, and Janna looked at him cautiously. He seemed so tired and discouraged that she felt the urge to stroke his cheek and murmur words of comfort, but instead she clenched her hands in her lap.

"I owe Zeke Bower the loyalty I'd give my own father if he were still alive," Cal went on. "And he's in very serious danger right now. I can't do or say anything that would upset him, and neither can you."

Janna faced him, her eyes wide and inquiring. Why did he owe Zeke Bower such loyalty, she wondered, and why was he telling her this?

"Several years ago, I faced financial ruin," Cal explained. "My father had just died, and I'd taken over. It was then I learned that Dad had made some bad investments and only a few thousand dollars stood between his estate and bankruptcy. I was responsible for my sister's welfare, too, and she's on her own with a daughter to take care of. Her husband was killed in an accident before Dad died. Anyway, to make a long story short, Zeke Bower loaned me the money to keep going and pull out of trouble. I've paid him back since, but . . ." Cal shrugged expressively, and Janna knew that Cal would always feel

176

in the old man's debt. And suddenly she knew more than that.

"He wants you to marry Lisa, doesn't he?" She said the words dully, seeing her future go tumbling around her.

"Yes." The one word said it all, and Janna turned her head sharply to hide the sudden tears that sprang to her eyes.

"But, Janna." Cal's voice was gentle as he reached over to pull her to him. "I want you to know that if things were different . . ."

"Don't, Cal!" Janna tried to pull away, but Cal held her firmly, drawing her into his arms.

"I can't help it, Janna," he whispered hungrily against her ear. "This may be the only time we'll have alone for a long time. And I want to feel you in my arms to store up memories to see me through."

"Oh, Cal . . . please!" Janna's words were muffled as Cal's mouth came down on hers. And then as he pressed her whole length against him, her protests died as heat suffused her body.

Cal molded her against him with warm, expressive hands, and once again Janna had the curious sensation that their bodies had been made to fit together in shared intimacy. She could feel every line of his lean strength against her, and she pushed her hands under his shirt to feel the warmth of his skin against her palms. Cal shuddered at her touch and lifted his head slightly to murmur huskily against her mouth.

"Tell me you love me, Janna. Tell me you want me. I want to hear you say it. I *need* to hear it!"

"Oh, Cal, dearest . . ." she breathed against his mouth. "You know I love you. And, yes, I want you. I want you so much!"

177

His mouth captured hers again, and now his hands pushed under her sweater to find her breasts. He turned his body to lean his back against the car door, pulling her on top of him so that she could feel his desire stirring against her.

Suddenly, he pushed her away and sat up. Janna was startled, still bemused and aching for more of his lovemaking. He lit another cigarette, and his hands were shaking slightly. Janna watched him through half-closed eyes, leaning her head against the back of the seat. She was tenderly grateful to see that she affected him as much as he affected her, and a mixture of confused love and bewildered resentment filled her mind at his actions.

"Tell me, Janna," he grated out finally. "Are you still willing to go to bed with me after what I've just told you?"

Cal's question hit her like a douche of cold water, waking her to reality, filling her with shocked despair and anger. "No!" The cry was wrung from her in agony. It came from hurt pride, shocked sensibility at his cruelty and a desire to hit back.

He laughed shortly with no real mirth. "No?" He looked her up and down hungrily, frustration shining from his blue eyes. "I think you're lying to yourself, little honey bear. But I'm not going to give either of us a chance to find out right now. Because once I take you, neither of us would let it rest there. I know it, and so do you."

Cal reached over and started the engine, gunning the automobile mercilessly as he pulled out onto the road and sped toward the cottage. He pulled up in front of it moments later and reached out a hand to stop Janna when she would have jumped out.

"Just remember this, Janna. You're mine! Don't get any

178

ideas of running away or of finding someone else to take your frustration out on. You belong to me!"

He let go of her arm, and Janna scrambled out of the car, shaken to the core of her being by Cal's words and actions since they left the Bower house. "I'll be back in an hour to pick you up," he called after her. "Be ready." With that, he threw the car in gear and took off in a savage squeal that kicked up gravel as he sped away.

Janna flung herself into the cottage, panting with emotion, tears streaming down her face. What in the name of heaven did he want from her? If he was going to marry Lisa, why was he so adamant that she, Janna, belonged to him as well? Did he expect her to hang around until the time came . . . and it would come, she knew . . . that he finally took her to bed and then expect her to indulge in an affair behind Lisa's back?

Janna stumbled into her bedroom and began to fling clothes into a bag, hardly knowing what she was packing, and even less if she was packing to leave here for good or to go back to the Bower house with Cal.

She had her cases packed and waiting by the front door before she settled down enough to think clearly. She couldn't stand any more encounters with Cal she was quite sure. As much as she loved him, she was not about to indulge in a hole and corner affair with him either before or after he married Lisa. And she wasn't going to leave Mr. Bower in the lurch either, she decided firmly. She was a grown woman. There would be no more running away. She would stay at the Bowers. She would watch Lisa and Cal together until the pain either broke her heart completely or she got over him, whichever came first. And she would stay out of his arms from here on out.

Janna felt as if she had truly grown up in that moment

179

of decision. And the mere act of making the decision gave her a sort of deadly calm that made her next actions and those to follow in the weeks ahead possible.

She took her bags to the little red car that stood waiting outside and climbed in to make the journey back to the Bowers alone. If Cal worried when he came for her, he'd find out soon enough where she was.

Arriving back at the large old house, Janna carried her bags inside and dumped them inside the door, then went in search of Lisa. The other woman was in an upstairs bedroom making a bed with ill grace when Janna walked in. She straightened up as Janna came to stand in front of her, and brown eyes met brown as they faced each other.

"Lisa, I've come to tell you I'll be staying only as long as it takes for your father to get well. Then I'm getting out of your life and Cal's. I'm telling you this so you'll stop treating me like an enemy. It isn't good for your father, and *I* have no intention of putting up with it."

Janna broke off, ignoring Lisa's astonished, open-mouthed reaction, and turned to survey the room around her. "Is this mine?" she asked crisply. And at Lisa's mute nod, she dropped her purse on a chair and turned to the bed. "Fine. Then I'll finish here before seeing your father." So saying, she began to finish making the bed where Lisa had left off. "I'll try not to make any more work for you or Mattie than is absolutely necessary." And as Lisa moved to the door: "I hope we understand each other now, Lisa?" Janna spoke quietly, keeping her features rigidly under control.

Lisa gave a trill of amused laughter. She seemed relaxed and free of animosity for the first time since Janna had met her. "Oh, yes, Janna. We understand one another. Obviously, Cal has told you where you stand finally. I could

180

almost feel sorry for you if I weren't so happy about it."
Lisa stopped at the door, her face glowing, almost gener-
ous in her relief. "And don't worry. I'll be as sweet as a
lamb to you from now on. I can afford to be, can't I?"
With another tinkling laugh, Lisa left the room, leaving
Janna to finish her task doggedly.

Oh, yes, you can afford to be, Lisa, she said to herself
with numbed detachment. You have everything I've ever
wanted . . . Cal Burke.

CHAPTER SEVENTEEN

Janna's days settled into a quiet pattern that made life *just* bearable. After the one episode where Cal had come storming back to the Bower house to find her settled there instead of on her way back home as he'd feared, he had left her alone, and that suited Janna perfectly.

She spent several hours a day with Mr. Bower, and a closeness had grown between them that tugged at Janna's conscience when she knew that one day she would be leaving him. But that was in the future: Mr. Bower was not recovering his strength as rapidly as the doctor had hoped, and there was no telling how long Janna would have to stay with him. Meanwhile, it was enough to sit beside him and talk for hours about her home, her past life . . . even about Frank. About everything except Cal, in fact. The older man returned her confidences, reminiscing about his youth and the years of struggle he'd had before successfully taming his land and making his fortune. He made no mention of Lisa's mother, and Janna sensed that it had not been a happy marriage. Perhaps that explained why Mr. Bower and Lisa didn't get along. Perhaps Lisa was like her mother. As it was, Lisa popped in for a short visit in the morning and in the afternoon, but she never stayed long. And as Mr. Bower seemed to tire rapidly during these visits, Janna found herself wishing that they would cease. Cal usually stayed with the old man for an hour or so in the evening while Janna had her dinner. During the day, he spent most of his time at his own home. Janna didn't know when he and Lisa got together, and she told herself she didn't care.

Mrs. Monroe was a competent nurse, and she and Janna had developed an easy camaraderie that made for a pleasant atmosphere in the sick room when there were only the three of them there. Mattie came in to change the bed linen and clean, and it was evident that she was fond of Mr. Bower—but that her real loyalty belonged to Lisa, Janna was certain. Mattie had been Lisa's nurse in childhood and their relationship seemed to be one of mother and daughter more than housekeeper and employer. Besides Cal, Mattie was the only person Janna had seen that Lisa seemed to have genuine feelings for.

Mattie grudgingly accepted Janna's efforts to help around the house, but her manner never warmed to the point where Janna felt the woman really liked her. But since Lisa did very little other than the shopping, Janna had quickly stepped in to relieve the older woman of what duties she had time for.

Emotionally, Janna moved in a state of limbo, only coming alive during her talks with Mr. Bower, and to a certain extent, with Bob. He came daily now to take her riding. As Mr. Bower had grown more and more fond of Janna, he had insisted that she get out at least once everyday to get some exercise and fresh air—and get out of the sick room. And so Janna and Bob had taken to riding horseback early in the mornings while Mrs. Monroe gave Mr. Bower his sponge bath and fed him breakfast.

Janna and Bob had developed an easy companionship

183

that excluded anything but friendship. And Janna was grateful that Bob had so easily dropped first his wish to develop something more than friendship between the two of them, and then his hostility once he had found out she loved Cal. Now he provided an outlet for her need to spend time with someone who demanded nothing from her except casual conversation without any uncomfortable undertones.

Janna was also grateful that Cal slept at his own home, so that she didn't have to suffer through nights of having him in the same house. Indeed, she saw so little of Cal that it was a shock one morning in May when he sought her out. She was washing breakfast dishes, and the weather was warm, so that she'd tied her hair away from her face and there were drops of perspiration on her smooth brow. She had on jeans and a white sleeveless tank top, but still she felt uncomfortably warm bending over the hot dish water.

"What the hell are you doing, Janna?"

The shock of hearing his voice after so long addressing her with suppressed anger caused her to spin around from the sink so suddenly that she splashed water from her hands onto the floor. After one startled look at him, she quickly turned back to the sink, but her voice mirrored her perturbation at his unexpected appearance.

"You startled me," she said irritably as she plunged her hands back into the water and picked up a plate to scrub it with unnecessary vigor.

Cal's voice was low and dangerous as he moved to stand beside her. "I asked what you think you're doing," he said persistently.

"I'm washing dishes! What does it look like?" She gave him an impatient glare and turned back to her task.

184

"I know that," he said grimly. "What I meant was, why are you washing dishes? That's Mattie's job . . . or Lisa's." The grimness was more pronounced now. "You've got enough to do without working like a slave in the kitchen as well." He reached over to turn her to face him, and his expression demanded an explanation.

"Mattie's got too much to handle right now, so I'm helping out, that's all." Janna didn't meet his eyes. She didn't dare. The touch of his hand on her arm was already awakening long suppressed yearnings.

"And Lisa?" he persisted.

"I imagine she's gone to town for supplies. I don't know." Janna pulled her tingling arm away from him and dried her hands on a towel. "Do you want some coffee?" She asked it mainly to distract him from the intent inventory he was taking of her appearance, his blue eyes smoldering with an expression she couldn't quite fathom. Janna knew she'd lost weight lately, and as she had always been slender, it was weight she could ill afford to lose. She didn't sleep well either, so that there were dark circles of fatigue under her brown eyes, and her hair had lost some of its glowing vitality. All in all, she felt she didn't present a very attractive picture—but then what did it matter?

"Yes, if you'll have some with me," was Cal's terse reply, and Janna decided against arguing with him, although she would have preferred to have left the room than to sit across from him with only inches separating them.

As she poured the coffee and sat down at the table with him, she couldn't stop herself from taking her own loving inventory, and she was dismayed at what she saw. Cal had lost weight, too, and his face was drawn into lines of weariness and strain. He was probably working far too hard, she thought miserably, handling both his own affairs and the Bowers' as well. Only his clear blue eyes were the same . . . and the firm strength of his hands where they curved around the coffee cup. Janna dropped her eyes hastily as she became aware that Cal was watching her study him.

"You look like hell," he said softly, and as Janna's head jerked up in indignation, he smiled wryly. "And so do I, I know. I wonder what could be the matter with us?" He was mocking her, and Janna flushed at the insinuation of his words.

"I expect we're both tired and worried about Mr. Bower. He's not improving nearly as much as expected, you know."

Cal frowned. "Yes, I know," he said wearily. "I've talked to the doctor, and he's not very hopeful. He says if it weren't for you, Zeke would probably have been gone by now."

Janna looked up, startled tears in her eyes. "Me?" She shook her head. "I don't do anything but talk to him. I like him very much."

"Yes, I know, Janna." Cal's voice was gentle. "But did you ever stop to think how much it means to him to have you talk to him . . . and genuinely care for him?"

Janna put a tired hand to her forehead to hide her eyes. She could stand up to Cal's anger, but his tenderness unnerved her unbearably.

"He has Lisa, Cal. And Mattie. And you . . ." As Janna said the words, the pain she felt slipped out unconsciously in her tone, and Cal reached across to take her free hand in his own, rubbing his fingers across her palm with disturbing effect.

"Yes. But I sometimes think he'd toss all of us out on

186

our ears if he could still have you," Cal said huskily. "And it's not altogether difficult to see why he feels that way."

There was a tight yearning in his voice that made Janna move restlessly in her chair. She tried to pull her hand away, but Cal held on to it, moving his grip to her wrist and running his thumb over the inside of it where her pulse beat erratically. Janna watched his hand as if hypnotized and then raised her eyes to his and caught her breath at the undisguised passion she found reflected there.

"Cal . . ." she breathed, unable to stop herself from drowning in that look.

"Janna . . ." He mocked her gently, but he stood up and pulled her up from her chair to hold her by her shoulders, looking down into her eyes still, then pulling her against him. Janna closed her eyes to hide her own arousal.

Cal put his arms around her waist and folded her to him with a firm, but gentle thoroughness. He didn't try to kiss her, and after a moment, Janna relaxed against him, content to rest in the security of his strength and warmth for as long as he would allow her to.

Mattie's voice calling to her from the hallway broke the embrace. Cal let Janna go reluctantly to return to his chair and his unfinished coffee. Janna picked up her own cup and was back at the sink when Mattie entered the room. The older woman stopped short at the sight of Cal lounging lazily in his chair, and her sharp black eyes took in the scene suspiciously.

"I didn't know you were here, Cal," she said almost accusingly, and Cal fixed her with a direct stare that seemed to disconcert her. "Of course, you're always welcome," she hastened to add. Perhaps she was afraid she had overstepped the bounds of her position by her accusa-

187

tory tone. "Do you want something to eat?" She seemed to be attempting to smooth over her earlier attitude, but Cal finished his coffee in one gulp and stood up to go.

"No, I merely came to tell Janna I need her help on some accounting matters this afternoon while Zeke's asleep. Can you spare her, Mattie?" He said the words in a dry tone, and his blue eyes lingered pointedly on where Janna stood with her hands in the dish water again. "I've done without her so long, the books have gotten into an unholy mess," he continued, ignoring the suspicious look that was back on Mattie's face.

"Can't she do it here?" The older woman spoke sharply, and Cal lost his patience suddenly and thunderously.

"Damn it, Mattie, no she can't!" The woman stepped back slightly at the vehemence in Cal's voice. "She's my employee, and the books are at my house. I'll be taking her back with me after lunch . . . that is, if you have no objections?" The sarcasm made Mattie shrink visibly. She'd known him long enough to know not to provoke him further when he was already very angry.

Mattie shrugged, attempting a nonchalant attitude that didn't quite come off. "I'm sure it's none of my business what the two of you do, Cal," she said somewhat stiffly, and then jumped as Cal banged his cup down on the table with a thump.

"That's right, Mattie. It damned well isn't!" Turning to Janna, he rapped out an unmistakable order. "Be ready at one o'clock, Janna. I'll be back to pick you up!" Janna nodded, not daring to dispute his ultimatum, and at that, Cal strode out of the room, every line of his superb body expressing implacable authority.

Janna was left with Mattie, and while she continued to wash the dishes, she sensed the woman's black eyes boring into her back. Taking a deep breath, she attempted to mollify her. "Cal looks tired, Mattie. I expect he does need some help, don't you?"

The woman merely grunted something unintelligible and left the room. Janna sighed wearily. She had no doubt that Mattie would lose no time in informing Lisa of this development, and Janna didn't look forward to the reaction from that quarter. But there was nothing she could do about it now.

Janna finished the dishes and got ready for her ride with Bob. She looked forward to his undemanding company and the relaxation of a ride through the beautiful countryside. It was a chance to get away from the sadness of watching Mr. Bower slowly deteriorate . . . and to get away from the uncomfortable truce that existed between herself and Lisa . . . and Mattie as well. Bob had never mentioned the subject of Cal or Janna's feelings for him since the day he'd brought her to the Bower house, and he was unfailingly cheerful and relaxed.

Janna met him at the corral where he'd saddled a roan mare named Lady for her. And as they rode over the rolling plains that were dotted with cattle, antelope, and wild flowers, Janna felt the tensions dissolving from her mind and from her body. But he must have sensed her earlier mood, for he was watching her more closely than usual. In an attempt to distract him, Janna exclaimed appreciatively at the sight of a female antelope with her young cropping grass not far from a small herd of cows.

"It always amazes me to see that, Bob. The antelope are so plentiful here . . . and they're so beautiful!"

"Yes, we have a lot of them, Janna. But if you ever get the chance to go to Yellowstone Park, take it. There are

189

a lot more animals there . . . moose, elk, bears . . . and it's a beautiful place with its geysers and hot springs."

"I'd love to go someday," Janna said enthusiastically. "And I mean to. You can stay at cabins right in the park, can't you?"

"Yep." Bob answered in his Western way. "I've seen Old Faithful blow from the lodge at the geyser, and it's a sight to see. You shouldn't miss it."

Apparently, Bob was either effectively distracted, or else he took her evasion in good part, for he didn't ask any embarrassing questions. They finished their ride in a companionable silence, and when they got back, Janna ran to the house to shower and change clothes before relieving Mrs. Monroe in Mr. Bower's bedroom.

Coming into his room later, she saw that he was so pitiably glad to see her that she felt an overwhelming sense of affection and responsibility toward this elderly man who'd become almost a grandfather to her.

"How are you today, my pet," she said cheerfully as she fluffed his pillows. "Feeling better?" Mr. Bower had had a bad spell the day before, and the doctor had to be called in.

"Not so's you can tell," he answered dryly, and Janna impulsively leant down to kiss his cheek.

"I'm sorry, dear. Would you like me to read to you, or would you rather sit quietly?"

"I want to talk to you, honey. Help me up a little so I can look at you while I talk."

"Do you think you should?" Janna was anxious about his waning strength, but he was adamant, and his next words shocked her.

"Janna, I'm on my way to dying . . . and I'd like to do

190

a little of what I want to along the journey. Now help me up."

Biting her lip to keep from crying out in protest, Janna helped the man to lift his frail body higher on the pillows. Then she sat on the bed beside him, holding his hand as he recovered his breath from the exertion.

"Janna," he said slowly, opening his eyes to peer at her intently.

"You're wasting away to nothing in front of my very eyes. I want to know why. Is it taking care of me that's doing it?"

"Oh, no! You mustn't think that!" Janna's astonished sincerity was apparent, and the old man grunted in satisfaction at her denial.

"Well, I didn't really think so," he said simply. "But there was always that chance, so I had to ask."

"Well, you can put that thought right out of your mind." Janna scolded him affectionately, and he smiled at her, but there was a shrewd look in the old eyes that made her uneasy.

"Then what is it?" he said quietly. "If it's not me, it's got to be something . . . or someone . . . and with a young woman, it's usually a man." He held up a peremptory hand as Janna shook her head negatively and would have spoken. "Now the man who's most successful at breaking the ladies' hearts around here is Cal Burke." Mr. Bower felt Janna's involuntary jerk, and it told him all he wanted to know. "All right, then," he said purposefully. "What's the matter? Doesn't he love you? Is that's what's wrong?"

Janna shot him a look of amazed disbelief. Surely he knew Cal was going to marry Lisa. Wasn't that what Mr. Bower wanted? She stammered, not knowing what to say. Finally, the one word came out.

191

"Lisa . . ."

Mr. Bower looked impatient. "Lisa's been after him for years," he said rather scornfully. "If he'd wanted her, he'd have taken her by now. She's no obstacle to you. She can't hold a candle to you!"

Janna's mouth fell open in astonishment. This was Lisa's own father talking . . . the man Cal wanted to please by marrying Lisa. She was utterly confused at the turn of events . . . and a little saddened by the fact that Mr. Bower had to feel the way he did about Lisa.

Mr. Bower eyed her consideringly. "What's this? Are you afraid to go after him because Lisa's my daughter? Psaw, girl. I'll soon be gone. Besides, I'm fond enough of Cal not to wish Lisa on him!" The old man snorted in amusement. "Oh, I know Cal thinks he owes me something because of a little matter that happened years ago." He stopped, and a calculating expression crossed his seamed face. "When's Cal coming today, Janna?" His tone was casual, but Janna had the impression he was planning something.

"He'll be here about one to get me," she said abruptly, and then realized the implication of what she'd said and hastened to explain. "He has some work to catch up on. I'm only going for a little while. I'll be back by the time you wake up this afternoon," she said placatingly.

Mr. Bower patted her hand. "Stay as long as you need to, girl. But send Cal up to me before you leave. I've got some ranch matters to go over with him. Time's getting too short to leave much to chance."

At the weary resignation in his voice, Janna became alarmed. "Oh, please, darling, don't talk like that. I can't bear it!" She choked back a sob at the realization that one day this wonderful old man was going to be gone from her

192

life. He wasn't going to get better. She knew it suddenly and irrevocably.

He smiled at her tenderly. "You *can* bear it, Janna. You'll have to. And remember, you've got your whole life ahead of you . . . happiness is waiting for you right around the corner. I'm sure of it. You'll get over my passing sooner than you believe possible now."

Janna shook her head but smiled through her tears. "I hope you're right, dear. But I can't see it now."

"No. But you will." He shifted uncomfortably. "I think I'll sleep until Cal comes. Stay with me until I drop off, then go make yourself pretty for him."

Janna helped him to lower himself down into a position to sleep, then sat quietly watching him until he drifted off into slumber. She was trying to take in the fact that Mr. Bower preferred Cal to marry her rather than his own daughter. Did Cal know this and was he just using the pretense of having to marry Lisa to please Mr. Bower in order to extricate himself from becoming too involved with Janna? Or did he genuinely believe that Mr. Bower wanted him to marry Lisa? If he did, Janna knew she couldn't tell him differently. Why should he believe her? And he couldn't bring up the matter to Mr. Bower in the man's present condition. So either way Janna was no better off than before she'd had this startling conversation with her elderly friend.

As Mr. Bower's breathing slowed, indicating he was asleep, Janna rose and tiptoed to the door. Mrs. Monroe was just coming in, and Janna put a finger to her lips to indicate quiet. The woman nodded, and Janna went to her own room.

Once there she changed into a denim wraparound skirt and a white peasant blouse, then stared at herself in the mirror with a dull lack of approval. Not much use in dressing up, she reflected dishearteningly. Maybe Mr. Bower was in her corner . . . and Cal's . . . but it didn't change anything. Even if Cal knew, Janna wasn't even sure he loved her. He'd never said so.

CHAPTER EIGHTEEN

When Cal arrived, Janna gave him the message to see Mr. Bower, and he disappeared up the stairs, moving slowly as if preoccupied, without the assured energy he'd always displayed before. Janna watched him go with poignant concern for the change in him. He must be so worried about Mr. Bower—as she was herself.

Cal was upstairs a full hour, and Janna sat in the study waiting, making a half-hearted effort to absorb the contents of a magazine, but not successfully. She was too preoccupied with her thoughts to concentrate on anything else.

Finally, Cal poked his head in the door, and Janna saw at once that his attitude had undergone a dramatic change. There was a light in his blue eyes she hadn't seen for a long time, and when he came into the room, his step was energetically confident and full of spring.

"What's happened?" she said at once, thinking he'd found Mr. Bower improved. "Is Mr. Bower better? Should I go up?"

Cal came to her and pulled her up into his arms without answering her, a familiar passion fairly blazing at her in twin shafts of clear blue.

"Cal?" She was smiling hesitantly, delighted to see him

acting like the old Cal she knew and loved, but curious as to what had caused the change.

"Yes, go up to him, Janna," Cal said seriously, but with a smile to match her own. "Stay with him every minute you can. We owe that old man more than you can ever realize . . . perhaps our whole lives." With that, he kissed her hard and then released her, moving quickly to the door.

"But don't you want to go over the books, Cal?" Janna was bewildered by his words and the apparent change in plans, but her heart was unaccountably beating with a light hope—more than she'd felt in some time.

Cal laughed gently and flashed her a possessive look that made her blush. "Not today, sweetheart. Today you owe to Zeke Bower. I'll collect what you owe me later." And with a wave of his hand, he was gone.

Janna stared at the empty space where he'd been for a moment, clamping down relentlessly on the happiness that threatened to swamp her good sense. After all, what had really changed? And while she was able to dispel most of her euphoric lightheartedness, the tiny persistent memory of Mr. Bower's earlier words beat a tattoo on her consciousness that wouldn't be denied. He said there was happiness in store for her. And he was a very wise man.

Two weeks later Janna stood in Mr. Bower's bedroom staring out the window at a dreary landscape. It was raining steadily, and the grayness matched her mood precisely. For nothing had changed at all except that Mr. Bower's condition had worsened to the extent that the doctor was calling in every other day. He had wanted to admit his elderly patient to the hospital, but Zeke Bower had been adamantly opposed to this. He seemed to know

196

that he had little time left, and he wanted to spend his remaining days in the home where he'd lived almost all of his life. The doctor's concurrence in this, even though it meant a great deal of inconvenience to his own schedule, served to convince Janna that she was going to lose her friend before too much longer.

That realization, coupled with Cal's failure to change any part of their relationship since the day he'd seen Mr. Bower—and Cal's increased solicitude toward Lisa—had sent Janna's spirits so low, it was all she could manage to maintain a facade of cheerfulness in Mr. Bower's presence during the brief periods he was awake. The rest of the time she did her share of the work and avoided everyone as much as possible. She had barely seen Cal, and Lisa was avoiding her father's bedroom except for one brief duty visit a day, usually when the old man was asleep.

Janna found it very hard to understand Lisa's reluctance to visit her father. Surely she was aware he was failing rapidly. But then Lisa was so different from Janna in so many ways, Janna thought they had nothing in common at all. With a heavy heart Janna felt Cal had a hard life ahead of him once he married Lisa. But perhaps Lisa would be different with him. At any rate she was always on her best behavior with him now.

Janna sighed and turned from her depressing thoughts to cross the room and sit beside the shrunken man dozing fitfully in the bed that dwarfed his thin body. As she watched his face, it seemed to her that he was having more difficulty with his breathing than usual, and there was a bluish cast to his features that hadn't been there earlier. With a muffled cry Janna was out of her chair in a flash, racing to the stairs to call Mrs. Monroe. The woman came at once, and after one look at her patient, she instructed Janna to call the doctor while she herself reached for a hypodermic needle filled with Adrenalin.

Janna's fingers trembled as she dialed the doctor's office, and she was frantically relieved when she found that he was in. She had been praying he wasn't out on a call. After obtaining his promise to come at once, Janna went back to the bedroom to find Mrs. Monroe taking Mr. Bower's pulse, her expression indicating the grave concern she felt. The woman had grown almost as fond of the elderly man as Janna was, and in his turn, Mr. Bower had gradually accepted his nurse with good grace and the charm he could exert so easily.

"How is he?" Janna's voice was not quite steady, and Mrs. Monroe gave her a bleak, sympathetic smile.

"I think you'd better get Mr. Burke over here, honey. And let Lisa know her father's had a turn for the worse."

Janna blanched. "Is it that bad?"

Mrs. Monroe nodded silently and turned back to the bedside again.

Janna stood numbly staring at the man in the bed who'd become so unbelievably dear to her in the past few weeks. Then with a choked sob, she turned on her heel to do as Mrs. Monroe had asked. Once outside the room, her only thought was that she wanted to see Cal. She needed his comfort and the strong security of his arms around her. Praying he'd be in, she practically ran into her bedroom to pick up the extension phone and dial his number. The ringing seemed to go on and on, and Janna had almost given up hope when Cal's voice finally came on the line.

"Oh, Cal, thank God. Please . . . you've got to come. Mr. Bower is . . ." Words failed her, and tears choked her voice so that she gave an almost inaudible gasp of pain.

"Janna, is he . . . ?" Cal didn't finish the thought, but Janna knew what he meant and she broke in hurriedly, trying to stem her tears so she could speak coherently.

"Oh, no! Not yet! But he's so much worse. And Mrs. Monroe said you should come . . . and . . . Oh, Cal, I need you so!" The tears flowed without restraint and her sobs were audible and racking over the phone.

"Take it easy, Janna." Cal's voice came firm and comforting, reaching out to steady her over the miles. "Don't let him see you like this if he's conscious. I'll be there as quickly as I can. Can you hold on until I get there?"

"Yes, darling . . . I'll be all right in a moment. And he's not conscious now, so I'll have a chance to pull myself together before I tell Lisa and then go to him again." The endearment slipped out as easily as it always had in her own mind, and she was not even conscious she'd used it. And a moment later, Cal's next words forced everything else from her mind.

"Lisa's here, Janna." Cal said the words quietly . . . regretfully? "I'll tell her now and bring her back with me."

Janna stood motionless, the pain induced by his words racking her mind and body, her world crashing around her and leaving her breathless in the resulting devastation. Mercifully, the agony passed quickly, and she was numbed to all feeling.

"Janna, are you there?" Cal's voice might have held a tinge of subdued anxiety, but Janna was in no state to pick up nuances now. Very quietly, with hands that didn't seem to belong to her body, she put the receiver down in its

199

cradle. Then, like an automaton, she crossed to her bathroom, washed her face to clear away the visible signs of her grief, and went to sit beside her elderly friend—a friend whose every tortured breath might be his last. And then she would be totally alone.

CHAPTER NINETEEN

Janna's numbness stood her in good stead the next few hours. Cal and Lisa arrived, and Janna watched almost dispassionately as Cal escorted Lisa to the bedside of her father, his arm supporting her around the waist as Lisa indulged in an emotional storm of grief that seemed remotely surprising when Lisa had heretofore been almost indifferent to her father's illness.

But nothing really penetrated Janna's shock-induced state. She had withdrawn into a shadowy corner of the room upon Cal and Lisa's arrival, and it was only as Cal led Lisa out on Mrs. Monroe's insistence that he caught sight of her there. He flicked her a sharp, all-encompassing glance that must have taken in the paleness of her skin and the unnatural stillness of her attitude, but he gave no other sign of recognizing her presence, nor did he offer her any comfort. Janna thought dully that he had his hands full looking after his future wife.

Then the doctor came, and Janna withdrew to her room to sit in a chair by the window and stare unseeingly out at the glory that spring had brought to the Wyoming countryside after the earlier rain.

She had no idea how long she sat there, but finally there came a gentle tap at the door, and she turned wide, frightened eyes to the sound, imagining that this was it. They'd come to tell her that Mr. Bower was gone. But as the door opened and Mrs. Monroe came in, she learned that he was still alive and was asking for her.

"How is he?" Janna asked. She had braced herself to hear the worst, but when it came, it was still a shock.

"The doctor says he only has a short time, Janna. He's lucid but is hanging on only through sheer will. So come quickly, dear. You won't have long." Mrs. Monroe gave her a sympathetic look and took her arm as Janna passed the nurse to make her way down the hall. But Janna was scarcely aware of it. She paused momentarily outside the door to Mr. Bower's room and took a deep breath, then quietly went inside.

The doctor looked up as she came in and motioned her forward. Janna could hear Mr. Bower's rasping breath as she crossed the room to kneel beside him and take his frail hand into the warm young strength of her own.

The old man's eyes flickered open at her touch, and a faint grimace of a smile touched the now cloudy brown eyes. "Janna?" he whispered hoarsely. "Don't cry." But the tears pouring down her stricken face wouldn't cease although she made a valiant effort to stop them for his sake.

"Like a daughter . . ." Mr. Bower got out, his words coming with increasing difficulty. "You're more like a daughter to me than . . ."

"Shhh." Janna couldn't bear to hear the words, because they called up visions of how unhappy the old man must have been if he could feel like that after knowing her for such a short time. How could Lisa have been so indifferent to him? But Janna hastened to reassure him that she felt the same affection toward him as he did for her.

"I love you, dearest," she choked out.

"I love you too . . ." Zeke Bower panted for a moment, and Janna looked anxiously over her shoulder at the doctor, wondering if she should go away and leave her friend to his rest. But the doctor nodded for her to stay, his own eyes moist at the touching scene he was witnessing.

"Janna." She turned her head quickly to catch the words. Mr. Bower's voice was very weak now, and Janna leaned forward to place her ear closer to his mouth.

"Don't worry . . . you'll be happy . . . I fixed . . ." Mr. Bower's sudden gasp and rigid straightening of his body made Janna cry out as she felt the doctor thrust her away to attend to his patient. She backed away from the side of the bed to cling to the post at the foot, gripping the wood so tightly, her hands were white with the strain. She couldn't watch the struggle that was taking place in front of her eyes, but she couldn't leave either. So she stood with eyes closed, one hand pressed to her mouth to stifle her sobs.

She was barely conscious when a strong arm closed around her waist and her hand was prised away from the bed post with gentle fingers. Then she was being pulled out of the room and propelled down the hall to her own room. Cal shut the door behind him and wrapped Janna in the haven of his arms, pressing her head to his chest as she cried and rubbing the back of her neck soothingly, all the while murmuring incoherent sounds of comfort.

Janna sobbed as if her heart was breaking—as indeed it was. For through the almost all-encompassing grief she felt at losing Mr. Bower, she felt the equally devastating loss of knowing that this was the last time Cal Burke would be holding her for any reason. The double blow was threatening to crush every resource of inner strength she

203

had—and so she let go of control and clung to the one immediate relief she had of tears in Cal's arms.

Gradually, her sobs lessened and she leaned weakly against the body of the man she loved, taking in deep breaths of air to try to bring herself to some semblance of control. Finally, she was able to straighten away from him, and Cal reached in his pocket for his handkerchief, then tipped her head up to dry her eyes with a gentle hand. Janna kept her lids down until he brushed her trembling mouth with his own lips, and then she opened her eyes slowly to see a tender light reflected in the blue eyes so close to her own. "All right now?" Cal's voice was husky and reflected some of his own pain at the loss of his old friend.

Janna nodded, not trusting her voice yet, and Cal moved his hands to her shoulders. "I have to go back . . . see if the doctor needs anything." He paused and shut his eyes for a second. Then he opened them to search her face. "Come lie down for a while. You're exhausted."

Janna submitted weakly as Cal guided her to the bed and lifted her onto it. Then he covered her with a spread and leaned over to smooth her hair away from her cheeks and forehead. As his lips pressed her temple, she thought she heard him murmur, "Sleep, darling . . . go to sleep now." And her eyes seemed to close of their own will in obedience to his words. She felt him move away from her as if in a dream—and that was all she knew for a long time. The blessed healing sleep protected her from shock, grief, and hopelessness and wrapped her in forgetfulness . . . for a time.

The sun was brilliant on the day of the funeral. Birds sang, a clean, sweet breeze blew billowing white clouds around in the clear blue of the sky overhead, and flowers nodded their heads in a symphony to spring. Janna stood to one side as the last hymn was sung and let the ambiance of the day and the occasion sweep over her without protest. She had reached a state of outward detachment that might have made a stranger think she was an uninterested onlooker. But anyone who knew her well would have noticed the pale translucence of her face, the lost hauntedness of her eyes, and the defenseless helplessness of her stance—and would have known that she was anything but unmoved or uninterested.

Cal stood almost opposite her with one arm around Lisa who looked quite beautifully tragic in her smart black suit. Her face was composed into a fixed sadness and there was a moistness in her brown eyes that charmed while it evoked pity. Friends and neighbors made up the rest of the gathering who'd come to pay their last respects to Zeke Bower. Janna didn't know any of them except for Bob, and he had merely pressed her arm comfortingly and then moved to stand with the rest of the crowd.

Janna heard the minister's dismissal, but still she stood, her eyes fastened on the mound of earth in front of her, even as the rest started toward the parked cars. Mr. Bower had cared enough to wish happiness for her. But Janna felt as if happiness were an unobtainable dream at the moment. She was only waiting a respectful few hours before she would be on her way to a lonely future. She didn't even have a destination in mind, although she supposed she would end up at her parents' home eventually. Meanwhile, she would simply get in her car and drive . . . perhaps to Yellowstone Park or Jackson Hole. It didn't really matter as long as she was able to lick her wounds

205

in solitude for a while.

At last she raised her head to see that the others had almost reached their cars, and she reluctantly stepped away after whispering a last good-bye to Mr. Bower. She would go to the Bower house for a few moments to pay her respects and collect her things, then she'd slip away to the cottage to finish her packing before getting on her way.

Cal had seated Lisa and Mattie in the long, black limousine reserved for the family, but he still stood by the door watching Janna. When he saw her move toward the cars, he slid in beside the driver, and they slowly pulled away down the lane toward the highway.

Janna followed the line of cars in her own red compact, and once at the house, she sat quietly for a few moments, allowing the others to enter before she joined them. Then she slipped through the crowd of sympathizers to climb the stairs to her room. It was a matter of moments to collect her things. She left a card of sympathy and good-bye addressed to Lisa on her bedside table, having decided she couldn't face speaking to the woman after all. Then she picked up her bags and left the room without a backward glance. She did pause outside Mr. Bower's room, but she didn't go in. She had said her good-bye to him.

The downstairs hall was clear of people now, so Janna quickly descended the stairs and left the house, grateful that no one had seen her. But her luck gave out when she reached her car. Bob came striding around the corner just as she was tossing her bags into the trunk.

"Janna?" He hurried to her side, looking inquisitively and anxiously at what she was doing. "Aren't you staying for the luncheon?"

206

Janna hesitated. Should she use this opportunity to say good-bye? Bob had turned out to be a good friend—and he deserved more than the postcard she had planned to send him later. She faced him and gave him a brief smile, devoid of pleasure.

"I'm leaving for good, Bob. I'm glad to have this chance to say good-bye to you. You've been a good friend to me, and I'll always remember you."

Bob eyed her with compassion. "I take it you haven't told Cal you're going?"

Janna ducked her head, unwilling to let Bob see the anguish in her eyes. "No. I . . . I thought it might be better just to go." Her voice gave a betraying quiver. "He's . . . he's very busy right now."

Bob shook his head in negation. "I don't think he'd be too busy to say good-bye to you, Janna . . . but I guess you know best," he added as he saw the quick flash of panic in her eyes. He hesitated and then said reluctantly, "To tell you the truth, I think you're probably doing the right thing . . . although once or twice, I've thought Cal . . ." He left the thought unfinished. "I'm sorry, Janna," he said sincerely. "You haven't had an easy time of it here. I wish it could have been different. I wish the two of us could have . . ." He stopped and gave a heavy sigh and then half-turned away. Then, as if making up his mind about something, he turned back to her. "You do still love him, don't you, Janna?"

Janna gave a somewhat jerky nod of her head and turned to get in her car. She didn't want to rehash her futile love for Cal, even with someone as sympathetic as Bob obviously was. Switching on the engine, she gave him

207

a last smile, wavering and sad. "Good-bye, Bob. Take care." And as she backed out onto the road, she saw him standing where she'd left him, hands in his pockets, a grim look on his face. Then he swung away toward the house, and Janna continued on her way to the cottage.

CHAPTER TWENTY

The air in the cottage was musty, but Janna didn't take the time to open the windows to clear it out. What would be the purpose—she'd only be there a short while at most— just long enough to collect her things. She went straight to the bedroom to collect the few items of clothing and other odds and ends that were still here, throwing them into a bag hastily. She wanted to be out of this place— away from the memories of Cal holding her, making love to her . . . hinting at things she didn't understand and he'd never explained, other than that he had to marry Lisa.

She snapped the lid shut on the case with unnecessary force and went to bathe her flushed face and wash her hands. She was debating whether to leave Cal a note when she heard the squeal of tires outside and then the slam of a car door, followed by rapid steps coming up to the house.

Janna knew it was Cal even before he thrust open the front door and came through, locking it behind him with a forceful click. Then he turned to confront her where she stood framed in the bedroom door, his body taut with tension, and his face grim. Janna swallowed nervously as he came toward her, and suddenly her palms were wet and her legs trembled.

"Cal . . ." she stammered. "I was going to leave a note

. . . to say good-bye." Her words were choked off as he grabbed her shoulders and pulled her to him so hard, she lost what little breath she had.

"Good-bye, hell!" He ground the words out in a thick voice, shaking her gently, but lovingly. "This is hello, Janna. A hello that's going to last us for the rest of our lives!"

He kissed her then, and Janna's head began to swim with the reaction he could always invoke in her. But underneath her exploding senses, and in spite of a dawning hope, she still needed words . . . so much so that at last she was able to draw her mouth away from his hungrily devouring lips and bury her head on his chest.

"Janna, Janna," he groaned huskily, crushing her to him. "It's been so long since I've been able to do that, and I've wanted to so much!" He would have kissed her again, but Janna put a trembling hand over his mouth. Cal didn't seem worried at the rejection, however. Perhaps because Janna's eyes were telling him so plainly how she felt about him.

"Cal, why have you come? Does this mean . . . ?"

"That I love you and intend to marry you?" Cal was grinning wickedly at her, but there was a seriousness about his words, too, that was unmistakable. "You know it does! And once you're mine, you just try this disappearing act you're so fond of and see how far it gets you!" He kissed her again, hard and thoroughly, and the denial of his emotions over the past weeks began to evidence itself in a rising passion almost at once.

Janna still had questions she wanted answered, but somehow they faded into insignificance as she began to believe in what was happening. And as Cal's hands and mouth took possession of her, the glorious feeling of leaning against the long, hard length of him blotted out everything but the here and now. It was a fiery heaven, but heaven it was, and Janna didn't want to come down to earth.

Cal swept her up into his arms and carried her into the bedroom, thrusting her onto the bed as if it took all of his will to break the contact between them for even the short time it took him to shed his clothes.

Janna fumbled at the buttons of her blouse ineffectively, unable to tear her eyes from the muscled brown smoothness of his shoulders and the dark hair on his chest that tapered to the waist of his trousers.

"Don't, Janna," he rasped huskily as the trousers came off and he lowered himself to sit beside her. "I want to undress you—it's my right!"

His fingers were swift and sure as they pulled the blouse from her shoulders and then moved to the buttons of her skirt. And soon, she was bare to the hunger in his eyes as he slowly took in the beauty that belonged to him alone. He lowered his head to her throat and kissed the vulnerable softness with heart-stopping sensuality so that Janna was breathless even before he started the slow, unbelievably sweet exploration of her body that was to introduce her to what it meant to belong to this man who already had her heart.

Before he stretched his length beside her, he reached over and removed the telephone from its hook with a purposeful glint in his eyes that sent a shiver through Janna having nothing to do with her nakedness.

"Now," Cal said, turning and sliding down beside her to take her into his arms. "Nothing on earth is going to stop me from taking what's mine—except you—and I don't think you want to stop me, do you, Janna?"

At his words Janna remembered Mr. Bower, and a twinge of shame hit her at the possibility of showing disrespect to his memory in this way. But when she hesitantly mentioned his name, Cal smiled at her tenderly and shook his head. "Oh, Janna—Zeke Bower would be the first to congratulate us on this occasion, as he would be if he'd lived to see us married. Don't you know we owe this happiness to him? And besides . . ." Cal grinned at her and kissed her with possessive thoroughness. "Zeke's motto was always to take what's yours and hold it and never let it go—and that's exactly what I intend to do right now, darling—with his blessing."

Cal didn't give Janna a chance to affirm with words the submission that shone from her eyes, as he suited action to words. And it was a long time before questions of any kind occurred to Janna—and when they did, the most important one of all was answered entirely to her satisfaction.

CHAPTER TWENTY-ONE

Jackson Lake sparkled in the sunlight, and the Grand Tetons rose majestically in the background to create a view Janna knew she would never forget. Cal lazily paddled the canoe through the blue waters, and Janna watched him with loving pride and then glanced down at the glittering diamond nestling against the plain band of gold on the third finger of her left hand. Happiness flooded through her in a tide of joy as she looked at the wind-tousled blackness of her new husband's hair where it framed the tanned strength of his familiar face. Her soft brown eyes were caught by two gleaming blue ones, as Cal observed her with satisfied possessiveness.

"Happy?" He was smiling at her with lazy contentment, and Janna's eyes shifted to the firm, sensuous mouth that could coax her to heights of passion she'd never dreamed existed.

"Absolutely," she answered him unequivocally, smiling in her turn at the relaxed confidence he emanated. He'd known what her answer would be before he'd asked the question.

"You'd better be," he growled in mock seriousness. "Because you're never going to get the chance to find out what it's like without me around trying to keep you that way."

"Suits me," she said simply, but she gave him a long intimate look that belied the simplicity of her words. Cal stopped paddling momentarily when he saw that look.

"Careful, honey bear," he said softly. "Unless you want the experience of making love in a canoe? I'm not made of stone, you know."

Janna knew that very well, much to her delight. "Ummm," she teased him. "Sounds wonderful . . . if a little chilly," she giggled at his raised eyebrows. Though it was June, spring in the mountains came late, and the breeze that blew across the water was very cold.

Another canoe occupied by a man and a woman passed them then, and the dark beauty of the woman reminded Janna of Lisa. She sobered just a little, remembering the venom that had exploded from Lisa Bower when she'd found out Cal and Janna were going to be married.

"I wonder how Lisa's enjoying Italy," she said casually, trying to sound unconcerned, but failing to conceal the touch of anxiety she still felt. Cal shrugged, his glance sharpening as he saw the disturbance on Janna's face. "I wouldn't know," he replied firmly, "and what's more, I don't care. I've told you I never loved her, Janna. Don't you believe me yet?"

Janna sighed, and her eyes were trusting as she answered him. "I believe you, darling. It's just that I was so unhappy while you were playing out that charade for Mr. Bower's benefit."

Cal frowned. "You weren't the only one," he said forcefully. But I admit I had it easier than you did. At least I knew exactly what I was doing—and who I intended to end up with." He grinned at her then with a touch of his old arrogance.

Janna wrinkled her nose at him. "You can't have been that sure I was in love with you—or that I'd stick around long enough for your plans to work out." Her tone was mildly indignant, but nothing could conceal the love in her eyes.

"Oh, but you were as transparent as glass, my love. I only had to touch you to know how you felt." Cal laughed at her expression of offended pride, but his manner was tenderly indulgent. "I never had a doubt in my mind on that score. In fact, I think I knew it before you did." He ignored Janna's uptilted nose. "But as to your sticking around, you did give me a turn or two. I was afraid every time you were out of my sight that you'd slip off, but even if you had, I'd have come after you." His complacent male determination sparked her off somewhat.

"Well, there would have been no danger of that if you'd have taken me into your confidence a little," she said somewhat huffily. "I still don't see why you couldn't have told me how you felt about me. It was downright cruel the way you let me believe you were going to marry Lisa at the same time as you were trying to seduce me." Soft color heightened the loveliness of Janna's face as she remembered the times Cal had almost succeeded in that seduction—with her own willing compliance! "I thought all you wanted from me was . . ." She blushed at his knowing grin. It was incredible, but she was still a little shy of him!

"You thought I just wanted to go to bed with you, hmmm?" He smiled crookedly, curving his mouth into a tantalizing line. "Well, and so I did want to bed you, my lovely wife—that was the only way I could be sure of keeping you with me. I knew your character, you see." Cal

215

suddenly pulled the oars inboard and came to sit beside her, letting the boat drift where it might. Janna moved to give him room after a quick look around assured her there was no danger. He pulled her into the curve of his arm and gave her a lingering kiss, and then looked deeply into her eyes.

"But that's not all I wanted from you, as you ought to know by now. I just needed time to make sure our love wouldn't hurt Mr. Bower. And if I'd told you how I felt, I didn't think you could keep from showing what was between us. A woman in love who knows her love is returned has a certain look—if I had a mirror, I'd show you!" Cal smiled down at the sparkle in Janna's eyes, and moved his hand to the bare skin of her waist under her sweater, stroking the satiny smoothness as he continued with his explanation.

"Even after Mr. Bower finally told me he hadn't the least desire for me to shackle myself to Lisa—and that's exactly the way he put it—I still couldn't risk letting Lisa know there was no hope of my marrying her. She would have been perfectly capable of putting pressure on her father to influence me—and in his weakened condition, it would have been almost criminal to do that!"

Janna stirred against him, distressed as always at the knowledge that Lisa could have been so callous toward the wonderful man who had been her father. "How could she have been like that to him, Cal?" She put her concern into words.

Cal shook his head impatiently, a grim expression on his face. "Who knows?" he said disgustedly. "I know he spoiled her when she was a little girl, but even that can't account for her selfishness. There's just no accounting for human nature sometimes."

Cal tightened his arms around her and tipped her head onto his shoulder, his eyes exploring the soft beauty of the face of his bride. "I *never* had any intention of marrying her, Janna. And once you came into my life, I knew it was just a matter of time before I'd have to make you mine—even if I'd had to hurt Zeke to do it. If I'd only known how he really felt about Lisa and me, you and I could have been married long before now."

Janna reached up to stroke his cheek with tender fingers. "Well, at least this way, I had a chance to get to know and love him," she said musingly. "And to comfort him when he needed me," she added. "If you and I had been married while he was so ill, I would have been so wrapped up in you, I couldn't have given him the time and attention he deserved." She sighed. "And it was a precious experience I can't regret even now."

Cal hugged her close to him and then let her go to move back to the oars. "Let's go make a camp fire and eat supper on the shore," he said firmly, trying to dispel the melancholy mood that had stolen over both of them in remembering Zeke Bower. Janna responded by giving him a dazzling smile.

"Yes, let's do that, Mr. Burke," she teased him. "And then if you don't mind, I'm feeling rather tired from all this fresh air and sunshine. Do you suppose we could have an early night?" she said with a false air of demureness.

Cal laughed low in his throat, instantly turning the boat toward shore. "At your service, *Mrs. Burke!*" he returned with alacrity, flashing her a look of aroused interest that made her laugh.

Contented, Janna sat back and gave herself up to the beauty around her. Cal's muscles rippled under his thin jacket as he pulled on the oars, and she regarded him with

217

bemused admiration, congratulating herself on capturing this man who must have had the female sex drawn to him almost from the cradle. The boat scraped the shore, and Cal jumped out to drag it up onto the beach, then reached out to lift Janna out, catching her against him instead of letting her go.

"Mrs. Burke," he murmured against her ear as his hands moved possessively over her. "I hope you've worked up an appetite for something besides food, because I've suddenly realized I'm much too tired to eat right now."

Janna laughed softly, her breath catching in her throat at the fire his hands aroused in her veins. "What did you have in mind, darling?" she asked innocently, tilting her head to look up at the dark face so close to her own.

"Why, a nap, of course, little honey bear," he said against her mouth. "A nap in the arms of my wife." He paused, raising his head to give her a look that melted her bones. "Just as soon as I've convinced the two of us once again that she really is my wife. And I know of only one sure way to do that."

Cal started toward their cabin, his arm holding Janna close to his side, and Janna went with him gladly. She glanced around her at nature's beauty, thinking that there couldn't be a better place to experience the glory of belonging to Cal Burke. And as the cabin door closed behind them, she reached out for that glory with every fiber of her being.

Love—the way you want it!

Candlelight Romances

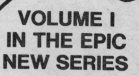

Danielle Steel

AMERICA'S LEADING LADY OF ROMANCE REIGNS OVER ANOTHER BESTSELLER

A Perfect Stranger

A flawless mix of glamour and love by Danielle Steel, the bestselling author of *The Ring, Palomino* and *Loving*.

A DELL BOOK $3.50   #17221-7